"Let me go or I'll scream for help."

Leo's smile dazzled. "And if you do," he said, "I'll tell everyone here that we're having a lovers' quarrel."

"None of them would believe a word of it," Tansy said tensely. "You and I don't go together."

"Don't be silly," Leo said softly, the words overlaid with ridicule. "They see a young woman so vital that sparks seem to fly from her, and a man who would give anything to capture that passion for himself."

ROBYN DONALD has always lived in Northland, initially on her father's stud dairy farm at Warkworth, then on the Bay of Islands, an area of great natural beauty where she lives today with her husband and an ebullient and mostly Labrador dog. She resigned from her teaching position when she found she enjoyed writing romances more, and now spends time when not writing in reading, gardening, traveling, and writing letters to keep up with her two adult children and her friends.

Don't miss any of our special offers. Write to us at the following address for information on our newest releases.

Harlequin Reader Service
U.S.: 3010 Walden Ave., P.O. Box 1325, Buffalo, NY 14269
Canadian: P.O. Box 609, Fort Erie, Ont. L2A 5X3

Robyn Donald
Tiger Eyes

Harlequin Books

TORONTO • NEW YORK • LONDON
AMSTERDAM • PARIS • SYDNEY • HAMBURG
STOCKHOLM • ATHENS • TOKYO • MILAN
MADRID • WARSAW • BUDAPEST • AUCKLAND

ISBN 0-373-11755-8

TIGER EYES

First North American Publication 1995.

Printed in U.S.A.

CHAPTER ONE

TANSY ORMEROD shivered in the frigid air blasting straight up from the South Pole. Although she'd had four years to get accustomed to the winds that buffeted Wellington she still found them hard to bear. And three weeks before Christmas it should be summer, warm and languorous, calling people to the beaches and the mountains.

Except that in New Zealand's capital nothing to do with the weather was ever so easy. The city's position on the southern coast of the North Island, open to the funnel of Cook Strait and the wild southern gales, meant that its reputation as Windy Wellington was well-earned.

'You're too thin. And born and bred in Auckland—that makes you a total wimp,' Rick used to tease.

'So were you.'

'Yes, but I spent my first five years in Christchurch. Now that's a climate you can get your teeth into!'

A reminiscent smile curved Tansy's controlled mouth. She hadn't expected to miss Rick. He'd been good company and she'd grown fond of him, although he'd only stayed a couple of months. Four months ago he'd gone to find his own destiny, leaving her surprised at the gap in her life.

That secretive little smile widening, she invited the passers-by to enjoy the mock-tragic ballad she was soulfully singing. Several coins landed in the guitar case at her feet, but not enough. Her gaze roamed further, beyond the lines of cars inching their way forwards.

He was back.

5

Few passers-by noticed the falter in her poignant small voice; the momentary lapse in concentration wasn't obvious except to her. That same large, discreetly opulent car, with the same man driving it, had sat opposite her for almost an hour on each of the last three days.

Of course, it meant nothing. Danger here came from people as poor as she, people who preyed on the buskers, not dark men with hard-edged, haughty profiles who could afford cars like that. It was just a coincidence. Perhaps he thought she was haunting him!

The last chords on her battered guitar summoned a smattering of applause, augmented by the cheerful clunk of coins landing in the case.

'That was a pretty tune. What's it called?' a middle-aged woman asked encouragingly.

Tansy's expression relaxed, although she kept a close watch on the money. Years spent earning her living as a busker meant she trusted very few, and certainly no one on the street. Yesterday her whole day's takings had been stolen when she went to the aid of an old man who'd had some sort of seizure close by. She'd only been gone five minutes, giving him first aid until others took over, but the money had disappeared when she got back.

She should, she supposed with a flash of acid humour, be grateful they'd left the guitar case behind!

' "Lament for a Lover",' she said, smiling.

The woman nodded and moved on. The person who took her place was big enough to block the keen force of the wind. Tansy looked up, one hand pushing back a straggle of carroty hair that refused to stay confined beneath her black beret. Her carefully impersonal smile froze into a travesty.

It was the man from the car.

That first shocked glance told her his presence wasn't one of the meaningless coincidences cities specialised in. Pale green, purposeful eyes scanned her with the cool mastery of a man who knew exactly what he was doing, and why.

Tall, quite a lot over six feet, which meant he towered above her five feet three, he was the sort of man she instinctively despised, all lean, languid sophistication in a pin-striped suit. Too young and too handsome to be a member of parliament, she thought snidely, using another professional smile to banish a clammy clutch of foreboding in the pit of her stomach. A lawyer, perhaps, or one of the businessmen who flocked to the seat of power to lobby discreetly for their particular field. Although something more fundamental and disturbing than the external indicators of expensive clothes and good looks, something that probably sprang from the unfaltering self-possession she sensed in him, sparked her initial suspicion into positive dislike.

Whatever, he certainly wasn't a civil servant.

'A very pretty tune,' he drawled, looking her over in a speculative fashion that made her bristle with resentment. Slashing brows the same charcoal as his smoothly waving hair gave him an autocratic appearance not mitigated by those chilly, perceptive eyes. He had a good nose for looking down, too.

A five-dollar bill was half concealed suggestively in his hand. Tansy's eyes flicked from the note back up to a mouth which, for all its beautiful shape, was set in lines that indicated an unyielding lack of compromise.

'Thank you,' she said stiffly.

'Have I heard it before?'

Her normally quick wits deserted her. In a flat voice she said, 'Often.'

'Ah, yes, in a couple of hundred folk songs about doomed love. I especially liked the tremor in the second verse. It made every woman go all misty-eyed. Who wrote it?'

'I did,' she snapped, brown eyes suddenly transformed by glittering sparks.

Anybody with more than a smattering of musical knowledge would have recognised the song for the pastiche it was, which made her grudging respect unnecessary. Anyway, she didn't have time to bandy words with him now. Unless fifty dollars ended up in the guitar case before the end of the day she'd be late with the rent again.

If this was an attempt to pick her up, she simply wasn't interested. As a prelude to dismissal she let her glance drift past the rangy, athletic body, and positioned herself to begin another song.

'Clever girl,' he said enigmatically. Then, so swiftly that she didn't for a moment realise what he'd said, he asked, 'Did you write it for Ricky Dacre?'

Normally sallow, Tansy felt the last tiny hint of colour vanish from her skin.

Although she had learned how to deal with anything the streets were likely to throw at her, there was a latent threat in the stranger's brilliant eyes and chiselled, angular features that tightened the muscles in Tansy's throat. He might look like some city sophisticate, but a hard determination transmuted the good-looking face.

'Who are you?' she asked quietly, because it would be useless to deny any knowledge of Rick. This man was here for a purpose.

'I'm his brother.'

Tansy had to clench her jaw to stop her mouth falling open. So this was Leo Dacre! Hastily regrouping her forces, she tried to impose a blank inscrutability on her sharp features, and knew she succeeded in looking merely mulish.

'Ah, I see you know who I am.'

'Yes,' she admitted. Rick had spoken obsessively about the man he loved and hated, the man he had, in a way, run away from. 'I know Rick has a brother called Leo.'

The black brows lifted. Not giving an inch, Tansy stared back.

Silently, he took out an ID card of some sort; below a photograph—a good one—of him, was his name. Leo James Dacre, aged twenty-eight. Going on a hundred, she thought sourly, nodding. There was no resemblance to his brother. In spite of everything, Rick had had a fresh, newly hatched quality, an essential boyishness. This man had been born worldly.

He replaced the card. 'I want to talk to you about him.'

Something about Leo Dacre sent icy little intimations of fear jagging through her. He was not, however, a man it would be politic to antagonise. Shrugging, Tansy said, 'All right, but not now.'

He looked down at the coins in the guitar case. 'How much will it cost me to buy you for as long as it takes?'

His words, delivered with crisp confidence, were inherently insulting, but only the studied watchfulness in his eyes revealed that he had used them deliberately.

Stupidly, because crossing swords with this man was dangerous, Tansy set her jaw and said with cold precision, 'You can't buy me.'

'Then I'd like to rent you for a little while.'

That was just as offensive. Obscurely convinced that revealing how angry she was would hand him an advantage she'd later regret, she subdued her resentment. 'How long will it take?'

'That,' he replied with an intonation that imbued the words with a threatening undertone, 'depends entirely on you.'

Tansy made up her mind. Although she didn't want anything to do with this man, experience had taught her that there were people you didn't mess with. Rick's half-brother was definitely one of these. It went against the grain, but she said brusquely, 'I need fifty dollars.'

If he'd shown any triumph or even satisfaction she'd have changed her mind immediately. However, his face was impassive as he drew out a wallet and handed her some folded notes. Deliberately, Tansy counted the money before bending over to scoop up the coins in the guitar case. When she'd packed away the guitar she said with what she hoped was distant self-possession, 'There's a pub just down the street.'

'How old are you?' He held out an imperative hand for the guitar.

Astonished, Tansy handed it over before she had time to think. 'Nineteen.'

Her twentieth birthday, which would have made her presence in the bar legal, was in a couple of days' time, but she wasn't going to tell him that, although she did say, 'I don't drink alcohol, and if anyone asks you can say you're my guardian.'

He swung into place beside her, cutting her off from the people who swirled past. 'I feel a little too young to be a guardian,' he said. 'How about a husband?'

Tansy's mouth, firmly disciplined to hide the vulnerability that was a dead giveaway, quirked into an unwilling, mocking smile. 'Not my type,' she said.

If she hadn't already realised that instinctively, the glances they got as they walked down the street would have told her. Most women did a double take when they saw the man beside her, eyeing him with interest and an unmistakable, primal response. Then their eyes switched to her, and that feminine alertness was replaced by surprise and amusement, even a slight smugness. A woman dressed in charity-shop clothes just didn't *go* with a man who looked as though he had spent more on his tailor than she saw in a year!

He looked over her head into a shop window, checking out her reflection. 'True.'

The speculative note beneath the word chafed her nerves. Pride lifted her chin, straightened her shoulders. She wasn't going to let this man make her feel inferior.

'No one will ask,' she said laconically.

No one did. Sipping the milk she ordered while he paid for it and the beer he chose for himself, Tansy waited for him to ask questions, wondering at a fatalism that sat oddly with her perception of herself. Surrender was not her style, but something beyond logic warned her there was no escaping this man.

'How long were you and Ricky living together?' Leo Dacre asked in his beautiful, cool voice.

Tansy bristled. 'We shared a room for a couple of months,' she retorted, clipping the words.

'And where is he now?'

Without hesitation she lied, 'I don't know.'

He let the silence drag out into tension before saying pleasantly, 'It would be well worth your while to tell me.'

Tansy hoped no sign of her inner turmoil showed. Although Rick hadn't boasted, from his conversation and reactions it had been obvious that the Dacres had had money for generations. With no income beyond what she earned busking, Tansy considered other things besides money to be important; loyalty, for one.

'I don't know,' she repeated stonily.

'That's a pity.'

Matching him stare for stare, she noticed an irregular, gold star around the pupil of each eye. It gave her a faint, uncanny chill, as though she were confronted by an alien.

In many ways, she thought, a glimmer of black humour lightening her mood, she might just as well be. Beyond common humanity, she had absolutely nothing

in common with the Leo Dacres of this world. An unwilling smile quirked her mouth.

'Don't you laugh at me,' he said evenly.

Captured by his eyes, crystalline and imperious, their
piercing clarity darkened by anger and will-power, Tansy
fought against an almost hypnotic compulsion to tell him
what he wanted.

'I can't help you,' she said brusquely, dragging her
gaze free.

Two very attractive women came laughing into the
room, their voices and posture completely self-assured.
Leo Dacre watched them go across to a table, his arrogant profile harshly forceful against the over-opulent
walls of the bar.

When he transferred his scrutiny back to Tansy it was
iced with offhand disdain, as though she wasn't important enough to get really angry with. The hair on the
back of Tansy's neck lifted in involuntary response; the
temper she kept so tightly curbed stirred and flexed. She
drew in a deep breath, applying the restraints and checks
she had learned, sending it back to its den.

'Did he tell you much about his home?' he asked, apparently idly.

Tansy shrugged. 'A little.'

'Then perhaps he mentioned his mother.'

She drank some of the milk. 'Yes,' she said ungraciously, 'once or twice.'

'They are—very close.'

Veiling her eyes with her thick lashes so he couldn't
see the indecision in their tawny depths, she hardened
her heart. Rick had worried about his mother, although
to Tansy Grace Dacre had sounded rather neurotically
possessive. 'So I gathered,' she said remotely.

'He can't know that she's desperately afraid and
worried, unable to sleep in case something awful is happening to him.'

Oh, he was clever. No hint of contempt in the dark, bland voice now, merely concern. If Rick hadn't talked incessantly about his half-brother, she'd have surrendered then. But Tansy knew more about this man than Rick, still starry-eyed with hero-worship, realised he'd told her. Leo Dacre was high-handed and unmerciful; he saw people as pawns to be manipulated.

'He was fine when I saw him last,' she said casually.

The magnificent eyes were hooded, like those of a bird of prey as it strikes. 'She has also just come out of hospital after a severe operation,' he said. 'Cancer.'

That was a bodyblow. But Tansy had made a promise to Rick.

'I'm sorry,' she said awkwardly.

'Unfortunately she has to have further treatment, and she wants him with her.'

'Naturally.' It took a real effort to keep her face set in an expression of mild sympathy. This changed everything. Although Rick might chafe under his mother's possessiveness, he loved her and he would certainly want to be with her when she needed him.

Tansy looked down at the hands clenched around her glass. Surreptitiously she relaxed the long, strong fingers while her brain raced, trying to find an answer to an insoluble question. What on earth should she do?

There was a balked silence, tingling with Leo Dacre's frustration. 'So you're not going to help,' he said.

He spoke quietly, but an inflexion in the smooth voice dragged Tansy's gaze to his face. A muscle flicked several times just above the tough line of his jaw. It fascinated her; her eyes lingered compulsively on the tiny betrayal, made all the more obvious because his face revealed no other emotion. Yet anger emanated from him in dark waves and she knew with a sudden terrible intuition that he was holding on to his control with a fierce effort of will.

'I can't help you,' she muttered, cross with herself because she was afraid. Striving to appear detached, she suspected she achieved a sullen boredom instead.

'How much would it cost?'

His callous emphasis on payment brought topaz sparks to her eyes. In her most offhand tone she said, 'I'm not interested in any money, thanks.'

'Don't make up your mind right away. Think about it overnight, and tell me tomorrow what your decision is,' he said, his voice warm and persuasive.

Tansy remembered that he was a barrister, a courtroom expert, with all the acting skill that that implied. She could see now why Rick said he was heading straight for the heights of his profession. He used his voice and his expression, his powerful presence, like weapons. In a courtroom he must be lethal; pity any poor witnesses who allowed themselves to be seduced by that voice and the implicit sympathy in his tone.

She looked directly at him, her shuttered eyes concealing the turbulent emotions that rioted through her. 'Sorry,' she repeated, drained the milk and got to her feet, picking up her guitar case on the way. 'Don't waste your time, Mr Dacre. I can't help you at all.'

As she made for the door she felt the intense impact of his stare right through to her bones. In its time Wellington had endured some awe-inspiring earthquakes, but the effect of that look, Tansy thought, trying to salvage some mordant humour from the situation, could well ricochet her off the top of her personal Richter scale. She tried hard not to be impressed.

Nevertheless, she noticed her boots took her across the floor faster than she wanted to go; she'd have felt better if she'd been able to saunter away, swinging her hips in a maddening parody of a sexy, come-hither walk.

Except that she didn't think she could. Tansy had learnt to blend in, and she'd tailored her walk accordingly, moving with enough confidence to be rejected as a victim, but without provocation.

Once outside she exhaled in a rush, looking around with bright, dazed eyes that only slowly took in the familiar buildings of Quay Street and the usual scurrying people. Presumably he expected her to go home now that she had her fifty dollars. So, adjusting her pointed chin to a jaunty angle, she went back to her patch.

All the rest of the afternoon as her fingers moved across the guitar strings and her voice flowed from song to song, she kept her eyes open for Leo Dacre, and couldn't have said whether she was relieved or disappointed when she didn't see him again.

Not that she liked the man. He was an overbearing, high-handed bully, with a fine talent for intimidation! However, it wasn't easy to banish an image of Rick's mother, ill and wanting him home. Although Rick found her unbearably clinging, he understood his mother's dependence on him. An inherited condition had almost killed him several times before he was five, a condition she had handed on to him. It had taken a miracle of science to snatch life from his living death, and years for him to recover and gain some strength. Horrified, his mother had refused to have more children.

He would, Tansy knew, want to be with her now.

What on earth should she do?

Still unsure when it was time to pack up, she struggled home in the teeth of the gale to her bed-sitting-room. Built under one of Wellington's old wooden houses in the inner city, it was within walking distance of the streets she worked and the university, which offset the higher rent she paid for its situation. On the floors above were a couple of flats with constantly changing occupants.

Tansy's room was small and dim, cold and more than a little musty. Sparsely furnished with a three-quarter bed and a chair that unwrapped into a single mattress, it had its own bathroom, if you could call the cupboard beneath the stairs that, and a tiny kitchen alcove. Not that she needed anything larger; her cooking tended to be just as spartan as her room.

All in all, the place was about as basic as it could be, yet Rick had fitted in quite unconcernedly.

Pulling off her coat and beret, she put them away in the cupboard that served as her wardrobe, and wondered caustically whether Leo Dacre had ever seen a place as down market as this. Probably not. Shrugging, she tidied the wild ginger tangle of her hair, eyeing her reflection in the mirror above the old chest of drawers beside the bed.

Her clothes were warm and clean, but showed their age and origins, and the maroon jersey clashed cruelly with her colouring. Like her wardrobe, the room was dominated by charity-shop finds, but the cushions and the pleasantly faded bedspread in subdued crimson and gold were chosen, as were the posters of South America on the wall, because their rich hues satisfied a hunger for colour and movement and drama that her clothes couldn't.

While the kettle boiled she checked out her bank balance. It made less than encouraging reading. In the past she'd always made enough over the summer break to pay her fees at university, but that wasn't going to happen this year. The recession was biting hard and people just didn't have the money to spend on itinerant buskers. Even if the rest of the run-up to Christmas was as good as it had been so far, she still wouldn't have enough.

And after Christmas, Wellington, like every other New Zealand city except the tourist towns, died over the summer.

Flicking the bankbook shut, she frowned. Now that her bachelor's degree was safely under her belt she was determined to carry on, although a master's meant an even greater commitment of time and effort for two years, and if the recession continued she wasn't going to be able to afford to eat, much less pay her fees.

When she left home her ultimate goal had been university. It had been a hard slog, and she had sometimes regretted her obsession, but a fierce, unyielding obstinacy kept her going. That same stubbornness compressed her mouth now; she had gone too far to give up.

After putting her bankbook away, she made herself a cup of herbal tea. She had survived before; she'd do it again. Some months ago, when Tansy was still sure she'd be able to manage, Professor Paxton had talked to a friend about a possible scholarship. Tomorrow morning she'd contact him and find out what was offering.

Slowly she reached across the table and began to go through the sheets of music she had left stacked there that morning. It was awful. Totally banal. Derivative. An ironic smile tucked in the corners of her mouth. Of course, she always thought that.

Did other composers look at their work and wonder whether they would ever produce anything worthwhile? Had Beethoven? Or Mozart? It didn't seem likely. As she drank her tea she scanned the sheets, hearing the music in her head. Then she made some corrections, and finally sat with her chin in her hand, wondering why she should be so convinced that her future lay in writing music. Not just songs, either. She enjoyed them, but they were ephemeral. She wanted to write music that would be listened to for the next hundred years.

Her eyes narrowed. It wasn't a matter of *wanting* to write; she didn't have any choice. Even if no one ever heard the sounds that filled her head, she would still be buying paper she couldn't afford and setting them down. It was a compulsion she no longer tried to resist.

But her heart wasn't in it tonight, and she knew why: Leo Dacre's arrival had thrown her completely.

What a mess! Rick had been utterly convinced that this was his one chance to wrest control of his life away from the demons that were driving him to destruction, and she had agreed. Still did.

Which was why she had lied to Leo; she couldn't let Rick down.

Nevertheless she felt like a worm. Even though Rick had warned her his brother would find her, she hadn't expected Leo Dacre to erupt into her life like the Demon King in a pantomime. And she certainly hadn't expected to feel that shiver of fear. She'd discounted most of Rick's endless discussions of his brother as adolescent hero-worship.

She'd been wrong; Leo Dacre was disturbingly forceful.

That was a mild way of putting it. He was an arrogant bastard with a cynical belief that money could buy everything. But did he know *why* Rick had run away from school halfway through the year?

She frowned, trying to remember if there had been any indication in his tone or expression. No; although that aloof, self-possessed face revealed very little, he hadn't appeared to know. Rick had said no one did.

And now Grace Dacre was ill. Tansy hated the thought of Rick's mother grieving and suspecting the worst, yet she still couldn't convince herself that she should go against Rick's wishes and tell his brother where he was. So much depended on it. Rick's whole future, in fact.

She chewed a moment on her lip. Damn Leo Dacre; why had he come and upset her comparatively serene life?

And how had he found her? Sudden tension prickled up her backbone as she wondered whether he had set a spy to watch her.

Not that anyone could force her back home now. That caution was merely a leftover from the time when she'd lived looking over her shoulder in case someone arrived to drag her back home.

Tonight at the café, she decided as she got up to shower, she'd ask if she could ring the camp where Rick was trying to put his life back together again. He wouldn't be able to speak to her, but she'd tell the man who ran the camp about this development. He'd be impartial, and she, cowardly though it probably was, would offload the responsibility on to him.

Three hours later she was sitting on a stool in the café when she realised Leo Dacre had followed her. The quaver in her smoky voice wasn't obvious, but she saw his quick smile and cursed herself for the small betrayal. Nobody else noticed. But then, her rendition of French songs à la Edith Piaf two nights a week was merely a background to flirting and eating and drinking and, during the university year, deep philosophical discussions on the meaning of life and the possible existence of a theory of everything.

Leo Dacre looked as though he was well aware of the meaning of life and had his own, perfectly satisfactory, universal theory. For a fleeting moment Tansy wondered whether anything ever shook that powerful self-confidence. Only for a moment. She remembered the tiny, ominous flick of muscle against his angular jaw, and felt another twist of inchoate alarm at the barely caged emotions she had sensed behind his sophisticated front.

But the fact that he was here meant that unless she could get rid of him first she dare not ring the camp tonight.

Avoiding his eyes, she smiled at the applause and went with smooth precision into the rest of the set. By showing up he was sending a message. She was, she realised grimly, in for a hard time until she managed to convince him that she wasn't going to tell him where Rick was.

Her life had suddenly become far too complicated. Perhaps she deserved it; anyone with any sense of self-preservation at all would have left thin, twitchy, obviously nervous Rick at the railway station that night six months ago, instead of taking him in like a starving stray and feeding him and keeping him warm and letting him talk to her as though his life and sanity depended on it.

Her voice lingered softly over the final silken syllables before trailing away into a plaintive silence. She smiled at the applause and slid down from the stool. Without looking at the table where Leo Dacre sat, she headed for the kitchen door. When it closed behind her with a soft thunk, her breath puffed through her lips in a sharp, relieved sigh.

'Brilliant as ever,' Arabella, who owned the café, said with her customary generosity. Large, flamboyant and in her late fifties, she was just outrageous enough to make it seem possible that it was her real name.

Tansy grinned. Arabella always tossed her the same compliment, and it didn't mean a thing. The main reason she was employed here two nights a week was that she looked the part; skinny and intense and soulful. Arabella thought she gave the crowded café a bit of Continental flair.

'Want something to eat, love?' The older woman inspected Tansy with a perceptive eye. 'You look a bit pale. Got some nice linguine tonight.'

'Your pasta is delicious, but I think I'll——'

Another thunk of the door silenced her. Prickles of recognition pulled the fine hair on the back of her neck upright. Arabella's dyed red head swivelled. After a comprehensive, almost awed survey, she beamed at the man who had followed Tansy in.

'Don't run away, Tansy, I'll buy you a drink,' Leo Dacre said.

'She doesn't drink,' the older woman told him throatily.

Normally her protective attitude amused Tansy, even warmed her a little, but for once she'd have liked Arabella to treat her as an adult capable of making her own decisions.

'Indeed?' He looked at Arabella, and smiled.

Tansy caught it from the corner of her eye. It was the kind of smile that could melt icebergs at forty miles: although deliberate, even calculated, its lazy, appreciatively male sexuality would take a far tougher woman than the café owner to withstand.

Arabella swallowed. She might have been planning to say something more but Leo Dacre side-tracked her neatly by murmuring, 'Not one of your vices, Tansy? But then, you haven't many, have you? You've led a very sober and industrious life.'

'Oh, you know each other, do you?' Arabella was openly curious.

Tansy opened her mouth to refute this, only to be forestalled by Leo. 'Yes, of course. Tansy, why don't you introduce us?'

Wondering whether that billion-kilowatt smile had scrambled her brains beyond redemption, Tansy did.

Within two minutes he had Arabella, no fool in spite of her soft heart, eating out of his hand. Had Tansy been less apprehensive, less tense, she might have admired a master at work. As it was, she could only fume at the unfaltering, devilish skill with which he soothed Arabella while implying without a word that he and Tansy were close friends and that, although he found Arabella interesting and sexy, it wouldn't be good manners for him to let Tansy see this.

He was clever. He was devious. He was beginning to scare the hell out of her. A man who could do that could turn her inside out and extract Rick's whereabouts before she had time to realise what she was saying.

Tomorrow, she decided abruptly, on the way to see Professor Paxton, she'd buy a Telecom card and ring the camp from a public phone box. In the meantime it would be necessary to keep a clear head, and not let Leo Dacre's smile short-circuit any more of the synapses in her brain.

'Well, Tansy's finished work for tonight,' Arabella said, obviously convinced she was helping an incipient romance.

With a last benign, approving smile at them both, she bustled across the noisy, sizzling kitchen to where her youngest son seemed about to toss a large wok full of stir-fried vegetables on to the floor. Arabella's cuisine was eclectic.

Tansy tried to pull away from Leo's hand at her elbow. He merely tightened his grip and guided her through the door back into the café.

'I'm going home now,' she stated evenly.

'Wait until I've finished my drink and I'll take you there.'

Her small, sharp chin angled up. 'I don't know you well enough to go anywhere with you,' she said, not attempting to hide the caustic undertone in her voice.

His smile was hard and enigmatic, green eyes the colour and clarity of peridots scanning her mutinous face. 'Of course you do,' he said. 'I imagine Rick's told you all about his horrible, unsympathetic, bad-tempered, far too demanding half-brother.'

Reluctantly, and only because she didn't trust him not to plonk her into the chair if she objected, she sat down. Her frown turned to surprise as one of the waiters, yet another of the owner's sons, arrived with a plate of linguine.

'No—Arabella's made a mistake,' she said, smiling. 'I told her I didn't want it.'

Leo Dacre pushed the plate towards her. 'Eat it up,' he ordered. 'No doubt the half-starved look is a professional asset when you're singing Piaf, but it doesn't do anything for your face.'

She didn't like him, she didn't trust him as far as she could throw him, yet the casual cruelty of his words hurt. 'I've always been thin,' she said stiffly.

'So you starve yourself to make sure you stay that way? Eat up, there's a good girl.'

Tansy hesitated. Leo nodded at the waiter, and said with enough command in his voice, 'Thanks.'

Waiting until Peter had scurried off, Tansy said, 'I don't like being told what to eat.'

'There's no sense in being stubborn merely for the sake of it.'

He was, of course, maddeningly right. Until that moment Tansy hadn't felt in the least hungry, but the steaming pasta smelt wonderful. Picking up her fork, she began to eat.

Tansy had a thing about hands. She believed they could tell her far more than expressions; people trained their faces to reveal only the thoughts and emotions that were politic, but hands and their movements were difficult to disguise.

Leo Dacre's were competent as well as graceful. They were also under control. He didn't wave them around, or drum them on the table, or scratch himself with them. Tansy found them distinctly unsettling.

Almost as unsettling as Leo Dacre himself.

A group of young men came in, shouting, laughing boisterously. Leo's dark head swung around, presenting a profile as autocratic as a king on a coin; he checked them out before dismissing them as harmless.

He was a barrister, Tansy knew, well on the way to taking silk and becoming a Queen's Counsel. Rick had been very proud of his brother's speedy rise through the ranks.

Leo worked in offices and courtrooms. Why then did he look as though he'd be more than competent to deal with any number of rowdy youths? Unwillingly, Tansy was intrigued. A good gym and a certain amount of dedication and sweat would give him the muscles that covered his long bones, but beneath the sophisticated, disciplined veneer she sensed something untamed and lethal.

He had a predator's focused awareness of his surroundings, a predator's skill in finding the weak spots in armour—look at the way he had charmed Arabella into submission, the way he had homed in on her own reluctance to make things worse for Rick's mother. As well, he displayed a predator's frighteningly fast reactions, and that invisible, potent aura of danger.

Altogether an alarming man. And she was his prey, the person that sharp, clear brain wanted to break.

For as long as she could remember, Tansy had singlemindedly aimed for one goal. She had sacrificed almost everything—a family, an easy life, even friends—for it. She had put herself in jeopardy, had learned to be streetwise, had gone hungry and cold for her ambition, and she had come to believe that nothing scared her any more.

But Leo Dacre did. Of course, she could save herself all this worry, and tell him where his brother was; she had done more for Rick than most would expect from a chance-met stranger. Unfortunately it wasn't in her to tamely knuckle under. And if she had been tempted, she'd only to recall Rick's desperate face and urgent plea to change her mind.

'This is my last chance,' he'd said just before he left, his determination as obvious as his fear. 'I have to do this, Tansy, and if Leo finds out where I am he'll have me out of there without a second thought.'

'Why?' she asked. 'Surely he'd be pleased that you're getting help.'

'You don't know Leo. He'd never find himself in a situation like this, he's too strong, but if somehow he did he'd deal with it himself. In our family Leo's the one everyone goes to when they need help, the only one who doesn't need help himself. He's tough, and he's brilliant, and he's got no weaknesses. People admire him, they look up to him. More than anything in the world I want to be like him. If he finds out where I am he'll take me home and make me see a psychiatrist, and it won't work, because he'll be there, he'll be watching all the time, and if I let him down again I——' He looked at her with such painful intensity that her heart twisted.

Then he said heavily, 'It would kill me, Tansy. If I can only have the time and the privacy, I know this will work. I can't cope with things like he does—I'm not as tough as he is—but I have to prove to myself and to him that I can do something right.'

All of his longing, the echo of years growing up in another man's shadow, sounded in his voice.

Tansy grimaced. She knew what was driving him, his need to prove himself. Her relationship with her foster-family had foundered on the rock of her inability to be the daughter and sister they wanted.

She looked at Rick's bent brown head and said angrily, 'Surely he doesn't expect you to be a clone of him, and if he is so insensitive, you're better off without him!'

'He's not like that,' he said simply. 'Just don't tell him where I am, OK? I hate asking you, because Leo's a master of applying pressure and you've been so good to me.'

Tansy laughed. 'If he finds me, which I doubt, he can't do anything more than ask. He's got no leverage.'

Rick eyed her with a grimness she now understood. 'You don't know Leo. He'll find something to threaten you with. But please, promise me.'

She'd promised. So, she thought, shaking her head at the offer of coffee, she would make sure that, whatever tactics Leo Dacre tried, she wouldn't give Rick away. He'd convinced himself that this was his last chance, and he deserved his opportunity.

A strange, fierce exhilaration flooded her. She would show Leo Dacre that she wasn't easily intimidated.

'Let's go,' he said, getting to his feet.

Apparently one of the tricks in his armoury was to take it for granted that she was going to fall in with whatever he suggested. Tonight she'd do that, for her own good reasons. Outside the bitter wind was now driving rain before it, and if she walked she'd be drenched by the time she got halfway home.

He didn't ask where she lived. She didn't tell him, but he drove straight there.

At the door of her flat he said, 'Are you going to ask me in?'

'No,' she said abruptly, bracing herself for an argument. Huddling a little further into her coat, she said coolly, 'It's no use, you know.'

Of course she'd known she wouldn't put him off so easily, but she was unprepared for his low laughter.

'I enjoy a good fight,' he said, a note of mockery giving emphasis to the words. 'Open your door.'

'I don't want——'

Ignoring her struggles, he picked up the hand that held her key and, with his warm one around it, forced the

key into the lock and turned it. His other hand came up
and switched the light on.

'All right?' He looked around her cramped domain
with eyes that took in everything.

'Of course it's all right,' she said, her voice rising
jaggedly. That swift, comprehensive glance was like a
violation. Defensively trying to block his view, she
stepped inside and swung around to face him.

'Right. See you tomorrow.'

He closed the door behind him with a loud click of
the lock. Automatically, Tansy put the chain across, her
eyes narrowed beneath her fine, straight brows as she
tried to work out what that had been.

Macho display? No, he had to know that men were
stronger than women. Was he proving that he could make
her do whatever he wanted to? Hardly. He was subtle,
not brutal and as lacking in finesse as a battle-axe.

He knew Rick wasn't there so it hadn't been that,
either, unless he thought his brother might have come
back that very day.

Was he concerned about her safety, for heaven's sake?

It gave her an odd little warmth, a warmth she instantly doused. She had lived on her own since a year
after she had run away, but even before that she had to
some extent always been on her own. Her foster-parents'
decision that she leave school and work in the local
supermarket had merely made obvious what she had
always sensed. So she had run away as far as she could,
determined to follow her dream and compose beautiful,
exciting music, music that would touch the hearts of
generations unborn.

And she had managed, with help, to survive. Chin
tilted, she looked around the small room, trying to see
it with Leo Dacre's eyes. OK, so she didn't live in particularly salubrious surroundings, but they were hers. If
she never produced anything more than the pretty little

songs she sang on the streets, she had made a life on her own terms.

But she *would* make music. It was a kind of rage in her, a need that was more important than anything else, more necessary than food, more vital than affection, more intensely satisfying than the most ardent love-affair.

It was her future and her present. She didn't regret jettisoning her relationship with her foster-family, and she'd not regret it if she never found anyone to love, because love could only ever take second place. There might come a time when she'd want marriage, and children, but at the moment she couldn't imagine it.

CHAPTER TWO

COLLAPSING bonelessly into the chair, Tansy sighed and pulled off her beret, tossing it on to the bed. Her hair sprang out around her narrow face like wildfire. It was, she thought gloomily, about the only thing about her that actually had any life to it. Too much life: completely uncontrollable and far too obvious, she kept it covered as much as possible. It contrasted brashly with the pale, scrawny, unobtrusive rest of her.

Suddenly weary, she got ready for bed, where she lay awake for too long, wondering how Rick was getting on in his self-imposed exile. And exactly what effect his mother's illness was going to have on his life.

On her way to Lambton Quay the next morning she tried to ring the camp, but was rebuffed by the very unforthcoming man who answered. He informed her he was the cook and that everyone else was out for the day, and as she opened her mouth, hung up.

'Damn,' she muttered, seething with frustration. That was several dollars down the drain. Hastily she rang the university, hoping to be able to talk to Professor Paxton about grants, but he wasn't there, and wasn't expected in that day.

Altogether an exercise in futility.

Just before lunch she watched a limousine pull up outside a very upmarket hotel and disgorge three men. One she recognised as an important industralist, one was a quintessential yes-man, dark-suited and eager, and the third

was Leo Dacre. He saw her, but apart from a quizzical
lift of his brows gave no sign of recognition.

Ignoring him, she hurried on her way, but the incident
dramatised the difference between them. King Cophetua
and the beggar maid, she thought ironically. Except that
the beggar maid had been beautiful, and the king had
fallen in love with her. Young as Tansy had been when
she'd read the story, she'd always wondered whether the
beggar maid had really enjoyed being queen.

It wasn't a good day; the weather was still un-
seasonable so there were few shoppers about, and those
who had to brave the wind weren't wanting to stop and
listen. At three-thirty she let herself think wistfully of
Auckland summers that started in November and went
on sometimes until June.

Remember the sticky, airless humidity, too, she told
herself, slipping into a rollicking Caribbean folksong with
forced enthusiasm. A few people tossed coins into her
guitar case. They were going to be the last; as she finished the song with a flourish she realised that the street
was almost empty of people.

Lord, she hoped things picked up. Perhaps she should
go north to Auckland. There were more people there.
Or Queenstown . . . there were always tourists visiting the
South Island's lovely lakes and mountains. And where
there were holidaymakers, there was a delightfully casual
attitude about money.

Unfortunately it cost money to get there. Of course,
she could hitch-hike.

No, it wasn't worth the risk.

She packed up and set off, telling herself that the odd
sensation under her breastbone was just hunger, not disappointment nor foreboding. The guitar dragged heavily
on her arm.

A moment later she decided that she might be psychic after all. A car drew up beside her and Leo Dacre said, 'Hop in and I'll take you for a drink somewhere.'

'I'm on my way home.' She was astounded at the treacherous warmth spreading through her.

'Get in,' he said calmly.

She shook her head.

'I want to talk about Rick.' He got out and opened the rear door, holding out his hand for the guitar. 'Come on, we'll have afternoon tea and then I'll take you straight home.'

And even as she wondered why he had such an effect on her, she found herself handing over the instrument and getting in.

'How long have you been busking?' he asked as he set the car in motion.

'Why ask me questions you already know the answers to?' she retorted.

He sent her a slanted look from unreadable eyes. 'What exactly do you mean by that?'

Exasperated, she glowered at him. 'Well, you obviously put a private detective on to Rick. How else would you have found me? And I'll bet you didn't just stop at a name; I'm sure there's a dossier about me somewhere.'

His hard-edged smile applauded her shrewdness. 'You're right, of course. Yes, I know you ran away from home and dropped completely out of sight for a year. Why did you run away?'

'Doesn't the dossier have it all set out for you?'

He ignored the sharp sarcasm in her question. 'Your family say you were always difficult to control, which doesn't match your reputation at school.'

She shrugged. 'My foster-parents and I didn't see eye to eye. I don't blame them; I must have been impossible to live with.'

'What happened to your own family?'

Tansy was beginning to realise that she was too vulnerable to this man; she needed barriers. And because she didn't seem to be able to keep behind the ones of her own making, she decided to hand him some. However, she couldn't resist asking, 'Didn't your detective find that out either?'

'He wasn't asked to,' he said. 'I know you were four when you went to live with the O'Briens, and that you lived in a social welfare institution before that.'

'My mother was a prostitute, I believe,' she said deliberately. 'She didn't look after me properly, so the welfare took me away and put me into a foster-home.'

She cast a challenging look at him, but to her surprise there was no sign of disgust or surprise in his face.

'How old were you then?'

'Eighteen months.' He might as well, she thought savagely, know the whole story. It had been a shock to Tansy when Pam O'Brien hurled the truth at her during one of their battles just before she'd run away; it would be an even greater jolt to Leo Dacre, brought up with all the advantages of wealth and security. 'She went off for the weekend with some man. Apparently a friend was supposed to come and pick me up, but she had a better offer so I stayed in the flat until the neighbours got sick of my screaming.'

He swore under his breath. 'Humanity can be incredibly cruel,' he said. 'Did you ever see your mother again?'

'No.' Tansy didn't want him to pity her. 'She died a couple of years later. I don't remember her.'

'If you lived happily with your foster-family until you were fifteen, what happened to change things?'

Beneath her jersey Tansy's shoulders moved uneasily. 'We disagreed on the course my future should take,' she said, not attempting to hide the ironic note in her voice.

'Some disagreement.' He waited several seconds, and, when she remained silent, said, 'So you ran away. How did you survive that first year on the streets?'

Tansy wasn't surprised his detective hadn't been able to discover anything about that year. She'd dropped out, living with a woman who'd made it her life's work to take in runaways and street kids. With a better knowledge of what could have been her future, Tansy never stopped thanking the fates that the tough, big-hearted widow had noticed the skinny, frightened girl at the railway station and taken her home.

Not only that; it was Mrs Tarawera who had lent her a guitar and suggested she busk for a living, organising an assortment of temporary sons and cousins as bodyguards for a couple of weeks to make sure no one stole her money. At Mrs Tarawera's house Tansy had learned to be streetwise; those same 'sons'—street kids and runaways—had taught her what to watch for and how to defend herself.

Mrs Tarawera was dead now, but she had left many living memorials in the people she had befriended and fed. Her kindness, and how much it had meant then, was one of the reasons why Tansy had taken in Rick.

And look where that generous impulse had got her, she reminded herself acidly, keeping her eyes on the road ahead as they drove up towards the Lady Norwood Rose Gardens.

'Surprisingly easily,' she returned lightly.

'I admire determination.' Skilfully, he passed a cyclist clad in yellow and black Lycra shorts who seemed hellbent on committing suicide beneath their wheels. 'Almost as much as I admire loyalty.'

She threw him a tolerant glance. So he thought he was going to be able to smooth-talk Rick's whereabouts out of her. 'Both are admirable qualities.'

'When not taken to excess.'

She picked up the gauntlet. 'Can one take—say, loyalty to excess?'

'Oh, I think so.' The car drew to a stop in the car park. As he got out, Tansy opened her door too. He asked, 'Are you radical in your feminist beliefs?' closing the door behind her.

She shrugged. 'Not particularly. If it upsets you to see me get out by myself I'm quite happy to humour you.'

He laughed, the brilliant, enigmatic eyes never leaving her face. 'I like the sharp teeth and claws,' he said amiably.

Something tense and forbidden stirred deep inside Tansy. A dart of sensation quivered through her, altering her, changing her in subtle, unnerving ways. Gazing around, she strove to overcome the unbidden weakness.

Rosebushes, although slightly battered by wind and rain, lifted valiant, colourful heads to the sun. Because the gardens were in a basin surrounded by tree-covered hills the scent of the flowers seemed to be concentrated into a ubiquitous, overpowering fragrance. The seductive perfume wound its way into her being, at once soothing and arousing her, so that she felt like a cat with its fur stroked the wrong way, wary and alert and reckless.

'Do you like roses?' he asked.

She nodded. 'Scented ones, yes. And the ones that are unusual colours.'

His gaze searched her face. She avoided it by stooping to bury her nose in one particularly rich, deep gold bloom, inhaling the sultry sweetness with pleasure.

'The bride of a friend of mine had all the roses at her new home dug out and replaced,' he said inconsequentially.

'Why?'

He was stroking a crimson bloom with slow, almost erotic gentleness. That strange feeling in Tansy's inner regions melted some part of her she had never felt before. Straightening up, she looked away, trying hard to ignore the image of the same leisurely caress on her skin.

'They were unfashionable,' he said, a sardonic note in his voice making his opinion clear.

Tansy said curiously, 'I didn't know there were fashions in flowers.'

'There are fashions in everything, if you have the time and the money to indulge them,' he said abruptly. 'Come on, let's go. I'm hungry.'

So was Tansy. By the time they sat down inside the kiosk she was remembering far too clearly that she hadn't taken time off for lunch.

To keep her mind off the man who sat opposite she let her glance wander around. Hothouse scents from the begonia house next door provided a striking contrast with the weather outside. Snatches of conversation, made piquant by their impenetrability, floated by. Tansy's eyes lingered appreciatively on the gilded, feathery fronds of a palm, the crinkly leaves of the low plants about its base.

Everything seemed brighter, with more impact than usual. Perhaps the scent of the roses had made her slightly drunk?

Leo said idly, 'Apropos of loyalty; surely it can be qualified by the needs of the person one is being loyal to?'

Tansy ate slowly, pretending to consider his remark. 'If I was sure I knew what they were, perhaps,' she finally admitted. 'I've always believed that most people understand their own needs better than anyone else, however affectionate or well-meaning the other person might be.'

Leo's mouth stretched in what was certainly not meant to be a smile. 'So you give yourself a good reason for opting out,' he said smoothly. 'I suppose it satisfies your conscience, but isn't it rather cowardly? Suppose you knew that someone was in trouble—would you just leave them to flounder along on their own?'

How much did he know? Tansy's gaze flicked up to Leo's face, but it gave nothing away, the regular features set into an inscrutable mask, his eyes like green glass.

Choosing her words carefully, she answered, 'Rick knows what he's doing, and that's good enough for me. Why don't you leave him to make his own way home? He will, eventually. He loves both you and his mother. Give him a chance.'

'To find himself?' His quick scorn and the contempt that followed made her shake inside. 'As you did? How did you earn your living that first year, Tansy? Prostituting yourself? Stealing? No, I don't really want to know, but do you want Rick to go through that sort of degradation?'

Mrs Tarawera had saved her from such an existence; when she saw Rick, as young and as frightened as she had been, her reaction had been instinctive.

Opening her mouth to tell Leo that his brother was not on the streets, she realised just in time how close she had come to betraying him. Thinking rapidly, she said, 'You haven't much faith in his basic strength of character, have you?'

If her recalcitrance irritated him he didn't let it show. His handsome face stony and unrevealing, he said evenly, 'So far he hasn't given much indication of any character, except a talent for getting into trouble.'

'Have you any idea why?'

'Oh, I've no doubt it's for the same reasons you left a perfectly adequate family. Unfocused resentment, a need to—where are you going?'

Tansy was on her feet. She had never come so close to hitting anyone in her life, and she had to get out. With a smile that showed small white teeth, she said sweetly, 'I don't have to listen to you rabbiting on about things you know absolutely nothing about. If you'd once climbed down off that pedestal and looked at real people for a change you might have been able to stop Rick before it was too late. Goodbye, Mr Dacre.'

He caught her up before she took two steps, his hand fastening on to her upper arm in a grip that almost numbed her wrist.

'Let me go,' she threatened beneath her breath, 'or I'll scream for help.'

His smile dazzled, a blatant contrast to the icy calculation that gleamed beneath thick lashes. 'And if you do,' he said just as quietly, 'I'll tell everyone here that we're having a lovers' quarrel.'

Tansy's mouth turned down. 'None of them would believe a word of it,' she said tensely. 'You and I don't go together.'

Taunting green eyes travelled slowly from the tawny flames of hers to the too-controlled mouth, and then down the pale length of her throat. Wherever that experienced gaze rested tiny explosions of sensation left colour in their wake, stimulated shivers along her nerves. An odd heaviness settled in the pit of her stomach, a melting combination of heat and hunger.

'Don't be silly,' he said softly, the words overlaid with ridicule. 'They see a young woman so vital that sparks seem to fly from her, and a man who would give anything to capture that passion for himself.'

The cold, cynical amusement in his tone hurt; it was like a slap in the face. She said clearly, 'Let me go, or I'll scream the place down.'

'Go ahead,' he said, urging her towards the door. 'This is the second time you've walked away from me. I don't like it.'

Opening her mouth, Tansy took in a deep breath. To her utter astonishment he swung her around, bent his dark head and kissed her.

His mouth was warm and compelling. Responses rioting into overload, unable to react because it was totally unexpected, Tansy gasped while he kissed her thoroughly and with flair, holding her so closely against his lean body that she could smell the faint but unmistakable tang of male, feel the hard, masculine contours against her.

She sagged, her slight body trembling. Instantly his arms contracted even further.

Through the ringing in her ears she dimly heard laughter and scattered applause, and then she was being picked up and he was carrying her through the door. She lifted weighted eyelids to stare witlessly at austere features emphasised by the taut skin across his cheekbones, an implacable mouth curved into a mocking smile.

When at last he stopped, she sputtered, 'I'll kill you,' scarlet with temper and humiliation and confusion. Furious with him for doing such a thing, she was even more incensed with herself for responding so violently.

He set her on her feet. The amusement had gone from his face, leaving it tough and forceful. 'Don't ever dare me again,' he said calmly.

'I was not——' Tansy's hands clenched into small but serviceable fists.

'Oh, yes, you were.' There was a note beneath the cool insolence of his reply that stopped her from erupting into a tantrum. 'I don't take kindly to being manipulated.'

With colour still stinging her skin, she stepped back, making a sudden grab at her beret. That unrestrained embrace had knocked it askew, and now the wind levered it the last few centimetres and carried it triumphantly off. Freed at last, her hair sprang out around her head in wild, defiant exuberance.

She seized a couple of handfuls and dragged it back from her face, saying violently, 'See what you've done!'

'What amazing hair,' he said in a constricted voice. Two vertical lines appeared between his brows as he scrutinised her. 'It crackles. Why do you keep it covered all the time?'

'Because idiots like you feel obliged to comment on it,' she snapped.

He grinned. 'It's hardly Titian red, is it?'

'No, it's ginger. Honest, unromantic, down-to-earth ginger. *Why are we talking about my hair*?'

It came out as a disconcerted wail. His gaze seemed to hold nothing but appreciation; it was as though those moments in the kiosk when he had kissed her had never happened. Except, she thought dazedly, a residue of the sensations his roving eyes and that firm, far too knowledgeable mouth had roused in her still seethed through every cell in her body, potent as cheap wine and just as bad for her.

'It's rather difficult not to talk about it the first time you see it uncaged,' he said, his eyes still fixed on the riotous mass. 'It appears to have a personality of its own.'

She flared, 'Don't you make fun of me.'

'Tansy,' he said with such relaxed assurance that she almost believed him, 'that is the most glorious head of hair I have ever seen. I swear I'm not making fun of you.'

Her astonished eyes searched his face, finding nothing but a bewildering sincerity. The anger and excitement and tension faded, leaving her flat in the aftermath of an adrenalin rush. 'You've got peculiar tastes,' she grumbled, looking around for her beret.

It was snagged on a rose bush. Jerking it free, Leo said lightly, 'I should throw the damned thing away. It's a crime to keep hair like that covered.'

'Don't you dare.' She almost snatched it from his hand, jamming it on to her head with defiant irritation, this time directed at herself. She had no idea what was happening to her, but she had the ominous feeling it was not going to be pleasant, and she wanted nothing more than to get out of there and away, back to her own life.

'Come on,' he commanded.

Tansy scowled suspiciously through her lashes.

'I'll take you home,' he explained with the patient tolerance of an uncle for a rather dimwitted niece.

More than anything Tansy would have liked to tell him to go to hell, but she wasn't in the business of cutting off her nose to spite her face. He had brought her here; he could do the decent thing and take her home.

'Very well,' she said ungraciously.

He didn't speak until he had pulled up outside her flat. Then, when she went to open the car door he said absently, 'It's locked. Tansy, listen to me. I can see I've handled this all wrong. Will you come to dinner with me tonight and let me explain about Rick, and why I need to know where he is?'

Tension stiffened her jaw. 'You've already done that and it doesn't make any difference,' she told him. 'I can't help you.'

His mouth compressed, but he said in the same moderate voice, 'At least listen to me.'

'All right.' Her lashes flew up in shock. She didn't intend to say that! A swift look at his hard, handsome face made her heart give a flip. Dicing with the devil was dangerous business.

'Good,' he said immediately, before she could take the words back. He did something on the dashboard and said, 'The door's open now. I'll pick you up at seven.'

'I've changed my mind,' she said.

He grinned. 'Tough.'

Tansy's face sharpened. She looked him straight in his alien's eyes and said calmly, 'Don't threaten me.'

'I'm not threatening you,' he said, sounding odiously reasonable. 'If you haven't got any suitable clothes, don't worry. I'll bring dinner with me.'

Oh, but he was clever. Tiny flakes of apricot heated her cheekbones. Chin jutting, her eyes steady, she said, 'Don't bother. I won't be here.'

'Then I'll come in now.'

Although he was smiling, Tansy sensed an unyielding determination to have his own way. He was going to say his piece sooner or later: accepting that, she accepted that it might as well be said on neutral ground.

Not that the kiosk at the rose gardens had inhibited him at all! However, if they went out to dinner he couldn't let slip the leash of his temper when she still refused to tell him where Rick was.

And although she didn't dare admit it, he fascinated her. When she was with him she felt more alive than she ever had before.

She said offhandedly, 'Oh, don't bother, I'll go out with you tonight. I can see I'm not going to get any peace until I do. But McDonald's will be all right. I haven't any formal clothes.'

His smile was twisted. 'Wear what you've got on now, except for that beret. People won't be looking at your clothes when they can see your hair.'

She shot him a last, fulminating glare, then got out of the car, slamming the door behind her. Unfortunately, it closed with the kind of solid heaviness that indicated excellent engineering and no damage done. Ignoring his laughter, Tansy stalked up the steps to her flat, her back held so stiffly her shoulders started to ache. Even safely inside she couldn't relax until the car moved away.

She did have formal clothes, of a sort. When the music department at the university gave recitals of students' work, each student conducted their own compositions. For those occasions she had assembled as near an approximation of conductors' clothes as she could find. Several forays through charity shops had yielded an oldish but extremely well-cut dinner-jacket which she wore with a white shirt and tailored trousers.

At half-past six she gritted her teeth and began to dress.

The severe lines of the jacket and the ruffles down the front of the shirt camouflaged slightly too opulent breasts, and her one pair of court shoes added the extra inch and a half she needed to give her some degree of confidence. For a change she didn't try to tame her hair. If Leo Dacre liked it so much, she thought, pushing a wilful tress back from her oddly flushed cheek, he could see it.

Except for a faint tinge of blusher along her high cheekbones and some gold eyeshadow, her skin and lips were as nature intended them. If she wore lipstick it made her mouth rather pouty and obvious. Her one luxury, the six-weekly dyeing of her pale lashes and brows, meant that her eyes were clearly defined. Fortunately they were large and dark enough to dominate a face that was too thin to be seductive.

Not, she assured herself as she turned away from the small mirror, that she wanted to be seductive. Not in the least. Brisk and businesslike—even formidable—was what she aimed for. Instead she looked short and slight and nondescript, except for her hair, which had enough character for ten people.

On the stroke of seven Leo's knock sounded on the door, and if she had dressed to please him she would have been rewarded by his candid, unashamed survey, the slow kindle of flame in the green eyes, and the half-smile that tucked up the corners of the wide, mobile mouth.

'Hello,' he said. 'You scrub up well, Tansy.'

The open laughter in his tone changed her initial re-action of fury and bleak resentment to a reluctant amusement. Stung because she was so easy to manipulate, she said, 'So do you.'

In a leather jacket over superbly cut shirt and trousers, he looked relaxed and informal, yet he was marked by an inherent sophistication that made Tansy feel suddenly young and very gauche. She was streetwise, he was worldly; there was an immense gulf between the two. Why that should disturb her she didn't know.

He opened the car door and held it with a teasing smile that invited her to comment. Tansy didn't. Once in the car, however, he didn't immediately start the engine.

Instead, scanning her profile, he said, 'Why don't we leave things as they are for the moment? I'd like to eat a meal without worrying in case you get up and storm away, or tip your plate over my head. I have to go back to Auckland the day after tomorrow; shall we go out to dinner tonight and tomorrow night, and after that I'll talk to you about Ricky?'

Say no, her common sense commanded her. Say no *right now* and go back inside and take off your pathetic attempts to look sleek and fashionable, and never see him again.

But something more fundamental than common sense prevented her from such drastic action.

Aloud, slowly, because she knew she was being stupid, putting herself in danger, she said, 'Yes, all right,' and comforted her sensible self by remembering that he was going away soon.

Besides, she reminded herself with a certain tough practicality that came from years of watching every penny, the free meals were saving her money.

To make things absolutely clear, she said brusquely, 'I'm only going out with you because you're paying for my dinner.'

His smile was cold and fleeting. 'I know,' he said.

That smile and the dispassionate tone of his voice sent a shiver tiptoeing delicately along her nerves.

He took her to a restaurant Tansy had heard about but never expected to visit. It was very expensive—part club, part café, and entirely fashionable—and she realised immediately that the unwritten dress code stipulated only that clothes be worn with panache. After several minutes she relaxed. She certainly wasn't the most outrageously dressed woman there by any means. In fact, she was one of the more conventionally garbed.

What she hadn't expected was the attention. Leo was clearly as well known here as in his native Auckland. After the third expensively dressed couple had stopped at their table, been introduced, and bubbled with enthusiasm and very cultured vowels at seeing him, she looked at him, lean and assured, sexy in a way that undermined her carefully constructed defences, and asked on a light note of provocation, 'Do you know *everyone* in New Zealand?'

'A lot,' he returned, his tone as casual as hers. 'I think I'm probably related to most of them. Both my parents came from very large extended families, so I've got cousins all over the place. As well, my father was active in public life. And I come to Wellington quite often.'

Which made it surprising that Rick had come here. Unless, of course, he had wanted to be found. More than once he'd admitted that he was very dependent on his brother, so perhaps unconsciously he'd been waiting for Leo to rescue him.

Instead, he'd decided to rescue himself. It had taken courage, and he should have his chance to 'find himself', as Leo so sneeringly put it.

'That's a very stubborn look,' Leo said softly.

Tansy's long lashes quivered. 'I'm a very stubborn person,' she returned.

'But not tonight. Tonight you don't have to be stubborn. Do you want to dance?'

A sudden deliquescence at the base of her spine warned her that dancing with him wouldn't be a good idea. 'Not just now,' she said. 'Tell me what it's like being a barrister.'

He looked surprised. 'Stimulating,' he said after a moment's consideration. 'Exhausting. It ranges from intense satisfaction to times when the world seems a wholly negative place. I wouldn't be anything else.'

Apart from her foster-father, whose only aim in working seemed to be the desire to make enough money so that his wife could buy the things she wanted, Tansy had little experience with men. Neither Les O'Brien nor the men she studied with at university were anything like Leo Dacre, who had a compelling magnetism that was unique.

From behind the menu she said, 'It sounds unsettling.'

'Don't you find life like that? Days when you think you can conquer the world, and other days when life puts you neatly back into your insignificant place?'

She was startled. It was difficult to imagine such a self-assured man feeling insignificant. 'Yes, of course, but I didn't think you would.'

'Why not?' Straight dark brows rose. He smiled at her swift colour and asked, 'Stereotyping me, Tansy?'

'I suppose I was,' she agreed reluctantly.

'I'm a man, like all other men. If you cut me, I bleed.'

A harsh undertone in his voice made her wince but she returned robustly, 'You don't have to convince me.'

'No?' He paused, his expression unreadable, then said abruptly, 'Tell me what you're doing studying composition in the music department at the university here.'

She shrugged. 'I think I was born making music. When I was a toddler I sang instead of talking. My foster-parents aren't at all musical, so it was lucky for me that

Pam, my foster-mother, used to clean house for an old lady who lived not far from us. She'd been a music teacher, and I think she missed it.'

She had shown Tansy how to play, and, when she realised how fascinated the child was, had begged to be able to teach her. Pam O'Brien had refused, citing lack of money, so Miss Harding had contacted the social welfare department. Some understanding person there had thought it a wonderful idea and organised the payments.

That had been the beginning of Tansy's double life. At home she had been the odd one out. At Miss Harding's she learned to round her vowels, discovered a whole new set of rules to govern her behaviour, listened with tears running down her face to the great composers, been made over for the best of motives into her mentor's image. But Tansy's happiness there, her sense of fulfilment, her eagerness to learn and desire to copy her mentor, set up tensions that eventually led to her flight from home.

'When I had piano lessons,' she went on, 'I spent most of my time trying to work out the theory rather than actually play the piano. I knew right from the start that I wanted to write music.'

Although forbidden to, she'd written at night, waiting until her older sister was asleep to work by the light of a torch. Of course, the inevitable happened; she was discovered. Angry with her for her disobedience, Pam had burned six months' work, so from then on Tansy had become even more secretive, losing herself for hours at a time in the special world she shared with Miss Harding.

Scrawny, intense, prone to temper tantrums and obstinacy, unable to compromise, she had been difficult. Like all creative people, she thought mockingly, she had suffered for her art. And so had her foster-parents. They hadn't been actively unkind; they had simply not understood her. Part of Pam O'Brien's resentment was due to the fact that she couldn't afford such lessons for her own children. It had been with a certain suppressed satisfaction that she had told Tansy one day in her fourteenth year that the old lady was dead.

After that things had gone from tense to impossible. She and Miss Harding had spoken of her future often, a future in which university loomed large. And she might have been able to go if she'd done well at school. But she hadn't—apart from high marks in music and maths she had barely scraped through her examinations.

Unfortunately, the understanding case worker had been made redundant, and the new one was inundated with work, and not musical.

It would be, everyone decided, a waste of money for her even to try, just as it was a waste of money to go back to school for the seventh form. So at the end of her sixth-form year her foster-mother had organised a job for her in a supermarket.

Left bereft by Miss Harding's death, with no one to counsel her, Tansy had run as far and as fast as the pitifully small amount in her savings bank had allowed her, ending up in Wellington because it cost too much to take the ferry across the Cook Strait to the South Island.

Although after that first year she had re-established contact with the O'Briens, she no longer felt like one of them. In fact, she never had. And she certainly didn't regret leaving; it had been the only thing to do.

'What sort of music?' Leo asked.

She shrugged. 'All sorts,' she said evasively.

'The ballad you were singing yesterday?'

'That was a pastiche,' she said aggressively. 'I lumped all the ingredients of a folksong together and came up with that. As you realised.'

'It sounded good.'

'Yes, of course it did. What's the use of singing a song if it doesn't sound good?'

'Particularly,' he said idly, 'if you want people to pay for the pleasure.'

'Especially then.'

'Do you like busking?'

She shrugged. 'It's a living.'

'It could be dangerous, I imagine.'

'I never go out at night. And there's a kind of cama-raderie among street people; we look out for each other.'

Frowning, he picked up his glass and tilted it so that the wine glowed as crimson as the robes and passions of ancient emperors. Lights edged Leo's features with gilt, throwing into high relief an arrogant line of nose, hard angles of jaw and cheekbone, the compelling statement of proudly poised head and clear green eyes. He was far too attractive, Tansy thought with a sudden stifled anticipation, and he knew it. That knowledge was apparent in his confidence, in the disturbing aura of leashed strength that surrounded him.

Looking up, he caught her staring. Gold glinted in the cool depths of his gaze. But he said casually, 'I don't like to think of you playing on the street.'

It was appallingly seductive to have him concern himself with her safety. Repressing her response, hoping he didn't notice the heat that swept along her cheek-bones, she said sunnily, 'Not accustomed to eating dinner with buskers, then?'

She waited for a throw-away comment, but he said very evenly, 'I'm not a snob, Tansy.'

'I'm glad to hear it,' she said. Of course he was a snob; he just didn't know it.

'For a woman who says she doesn't throw out dares, you have a way of making a challenge of everything you say. Now, we'd better discuss politics. You can't eat dinner in Wellington and not talk politics.'

It wasn't a subject normally discussed in her circles, or only as far as the government's activities affected the music department, but Tansy read the newspapers in the library so she was able to keep her end up in the minutes that followed. She finished the meal more than impressed by Leo's incisive intelligence.

He was a formidable man, she thought as she drained the last of her coffee. She should remember that. Rick had taken his brother's keen brain and uncompromising, concentrated authority for granted, and she'd probably made a mistake by looking at him through Rick's eyes.

This man would make a bad enemy.

'Dance?' he said, his lazy inflexion somehow allaying the apprehension that chilled along her spine.

Another sort of misgiving tightened her skin. The memory of those moments when he had held her and kissed her, when strong arms tightened around her and she had been pressed against the lean hardness of his body, was never far away. It would be foolhardy to risk that sort of danger again. Fortunately the floor was filled with couples who were boogying vigorously and apart.

'Yes,' she said brightly.

He danced stylishly, with a controlled animal grace. For once, Tansy let herself go. Most of all she loved to dance in a skirt, getting a sensual pleasure from the fluid swirl and play of the material about her legs, but tonight she was rather glad she was wearing trousers. She didn't need any extra stimulation.

When the music swung straight into another tune, slow and sensuous this time, Leo pulled her into his arms and held her firmly but not too closely. Tansy was breathing heavily from the previous dance, her chest lifting, the air coming hotly between her lips. With every breath, her breasts brushed against him. Before long she was devoutly thankful she was wearing the dinner-jacket and not some thin dress, because beneath the material of her blouse strange sensations pulled her nipples into little pointed buds. Shivery feelings spread in a complex web across her entire body, and wherever they went they left havoc behind.

It had never happened to her before, though of course she knew what it was. She had always believed people made too much of sexual attraction—after all, anyone with more than a pea for a brain and a modicum of self-control ought to be able to restrain their elemental urges.

Now, however, as she moved in his arms to the music, now she understood what all the fuss was about.

CHAPTER THREE

'YOU dance superbly,' he said into her ear. 'Graceful as a cat, and white-hot with energy.'

'It's the hair,' she said prosaically, trying to set him at a distance, trying to banish the secret thrill his compliment gave her. 'It has all the energy. One of these days I'll get it cut off.'

'It would be a sin.'

She smiled. 'It would have to be shaved,' she admitted. 'I did try once. It sticks out like a bush in a high wind unless it's weighed down by its own length. Little Orphan Annie had nothing on my hair.'

His laughter touched something deep inside her. She looked away, willing herself to remain detached. He was using his potent masculine charisma, flirting a little, softening her up so that when the time came she might forget to keep her promise to Rick.

She'd have to ignore the clamour of her senses, just as she was ignoring the tell-tale hardness of his body, the subliminal signals that bypassed her brain and told an older, more primitive part of her that he was not unaffected by her nearness. Men, she knew, were inclined to desire women quite indiscriminately. It had something to do with their hormones.

Picking up the tune, she hummed for a few seconds until, realising what she was doing, she stopped.

'I like your voice,' he said. 'You're not diva material by any means, but there's something about your singing that makes people stop. The way you sing, I think: so intensely—consumed heart and soul by the moment. And your voice is husky—very sexy.'

'Thank you.' If she hadn't known what he was doing, she might have been in real danger.

He added solemnly, 'You can carry a tune, too.'

Catching the flicker of humour in his eyes, Tansy laughed. 'Just as well.'

'Mmm. I suppose a composer would have to have perfect pitch.'

'It helps,' she said drily.

'Or do you do conceptual music—ten minutes of silence, broken by the occasional tinkle of broken glass?'

'Happenings?' She shook her head. 'No, I'm far more conventional. I want to make music that inspires and moves, that has an impact, music that brings tears to people's eyes. Like Vivaldi, and Beethoven and Verdi.'

'Not a small ambition,' he said thoughtfully.

'No. Sometimes I wonder how I have the cheek even to try.'

'How do you?'

She searched for words to explain the inexplicable even as she wondered why she was talking to him like this, as though she had known him for years.

'I have to,' she said in the end, allowing frankness to take over from the usual modesty. 'It's something in me that won't let me rest. The only time I'm really happy is when I'm writing music. And then I look at it and think that I have to be the biggest con in history.'

'But even if you don't get there you'll die trying.'

Tansy was surprised again. Leo seemed too sophisticated to comprehend the elemental need that music was to her, yet it seemed he did.

'Yes,' she said quietly. 'I can't help it.'

'So everything gets sacrificed to it.'

He understood too well. Yet sacrifice was the wrong word, because nothing else in the world gave her such keen, undiluted pleasure as her music.

'Perhaps,' she said non-committally.

'The first thing I noticed about you was that passionate, incandescent, driven look.'

She sent him a shocked, cautious glance. 'You must be getting me mixed up with my hair,' she said, automatically deflecting him again. 'It's got all the character and personality. I'm very ordinary.'

She had let him see too far into her; she should have remembered that he earned his very nice living by peering into people's lives and minds.

'I noticed it before you unveiled the hair,' he said, his voice cool and hard and uncompromising. 'One look from those tiger eyes, ardent and untamed, yet strangely detached, told me that you took life on your own terms or not at all. How did you fare on the street for that first year, Tansy?'

'Well enough,' she said distantly.

'It certainly doesn't seem to have left scars on you.'

She opened her mouth to tell him the truth, then closed it again.

At least some area of her past was sealed from his knowing eyes. The thought of her life being laid out before him in black and white made her feel sick; it was a violation, a psychic rape, a vulgar invasion of her privacy.

If she'd cared for his opinion she'd have told him that far from prostituting herself to keep body and soul together she had been safe and protected. But she didn't care, and once he was gone she'd never see him again.

While she'd been talking she had been able to relegate the unfortunate physical effect he had on her to the back of her brain, but he was silent now, and she was once more left defenceless against the tyranny of her senses.

Careful, Tansy, she told that weakening part of her. The honeyed compliments and that deft use of tone and touch are all part of his plan.

Too clever to be obvious, he was skilfully trying to seduce her. There was no crude grappling her against him with octopus arms, no blunt comments on how attractive she was, no suggestive looks or remarks, but he didn't try to hide the fact that he was aroused by her, that when they moved together the imprint of her body against his did interesting things to him.

Tansy hadn't thought she was afraid of anything, but she recognised fear now. Blind instinct was taking over from rational thought, her body forcing her to acknowledge its primacy; she shivered suddenly at the fierceness of the response that threatened her.

She should never have agreed to go out with him; it was unlike her, just another indication of how much he affected her. Leo Dacre was bad news.

'What are you thinking?' he asked, using the hand that held hers to tilt her chin so that he could search her face with those perceptive eyes.

Her lashes kept him at bay. 'Just enjoying the music,' she said easily.

His speculative scrutiny was difficult to parry. Tansy compelled her face to remain bland, faintly enquiring, her thin brows raised just to the right height, her expression placid.

'Liar,' he said, the golden stars gleaming with something that was almost certainly calculation, but he let her chin go and resumed normal dancing grip.

A soundless sigh of relief escaped Tansy's lips.

'You say more in your silences than most people do when they talk,' he said, his voice slow and smooth as cream. 'Why no boyfriend, Tansy?'

'I'm too busy.'

'And how did you get to be called Tansy, anyway? Your family call you Sherryl.'

'It's my real name. My foster-mother didn't like it so she renamed me. When I left home I changed back.'

'I don't blame you. But to the O'Briens you're still Sherryl.'

She smiled without humour. 'To my family I'm still an idiot,' she said flippantly.

'No wonder you and Ricky had a lot in common. Both of you with a ton weight of chips on your shoulders.'

'That can't be right,' she said, hiding an ache of pain at his harsh words. 'Both of us can shrug quite easily.'

A short pause restored some of her confidence. At least she could make him think now and then.

'So you can,' he drawled. 'In your case, with great style.'

Tansy's eye was caught by two people standing on the edge of the small dance-floor. They were a little older than Tansy, in their late twenties, perhaps; about Leo's age. And although their interested eyes passed without recognition over her, they obviously knew Leo.

Sure enough, somewhat to her relief, they made their way across the floor. 'Leo,' the man said, touching him on the arm. 'What are you doing down here?'

His expression didn't alter, and he greeted them with what seemed to be affection, yet Tansy got the impression that he wasn't particularly pleased to see them.

'Working,' he said laconically, before introducing them.

They were Simon and Paula Farquharson, and they were curious. Paula's eyes darted from Leo's bland impassivity to Tansy's face, as she said with a gracious smile, 'I'm sure I know you. We must have met somewhere, although your name doesn't ring a bell, I'm afraid.'

Tansy smiled. 'You've probably seen me busking.'

The other woman's mouth stayed open for a second. 'Oh, yes, of course,' she said almost immediately. 'That's it. You're on Lambton Quay quite often at lunchtime.'

She darted a swift glance at Leo, then smiled at Tansy with what she probably thought was urbane cordiality. Unfortunately it came out as bewildered—*what* was Leo Dacre doing with someone who sang on the streets for a living, for heaven's sake?—and patronising.

Sure enough, the woman said, 'I'm sorry, I should have recognised you, but I'm afraid I don't take much notice of b-people who play on the street.'

'Why should you?' Tansy said, rescuing her. Although her snobbery was irritating it came at just the right time. It made Tansy realise just how big a distance, in every way, there was between herself and Leo. 'We're there to provide a pleasant noise, something a little more human than the traffic. However, I must admit that some of us sound distinctly inhuman. I've never really understood what they meant by murdering music until I heard a certain sax player.'

Paula smiled and relaxed, but, although she tried to hide it, it was clear that she was puzzled.

'She thinks you've gone very downmarket,' Tansy said solemnly when Leo had refused the offer of a drink and the others had left them to begin dancing again.

'Did she get to you?' He sounded indolently amused. 'She's a silly woman, Paula, a bit naïve still. That's what a sheltered upbringing does to you. She'll grow up.'

'But is your reputation going to stand being seen with me?'

He laughed. 'I think so.'

His total confidence made her angry. With something of a snap in her voice she said, 'Of course, you don't really have to worry. Dacres are born with a silver spoon, and unless you skip the country with the contents of your clients' trust funds or take bribes, the reputation stays intact.'

'Reverse snobbery?' he asked, his narrowed gaze very green as it rested on her face. 'You're going to have to work on these prejudices you insist on parading—they inhibit creative spirits, you know. As it happens, very few of my clients have trust funds, and I certainly can't get my hands on them. I think you're mistaking me for a solicitor.'

Tansy could have bitten out her tongue. Rick had been inclined to go on about his family, how he was expected to do better than anyone else because that was what Dacres always did. Leo had been his role model, one he knew he had no hope of emulating. Leo was the strong brother, the clever one, the one who was respected and looked up to, the head prefect, the brilliant university student with an equally glittering career in front of him.

Did Leo know how difficult it had been for his much younger half-brother to live up to his achievements? Perhaps. He was astute, but even the most perceptive person could be oddly blind when it came to those closest to them.

'My family,' he said now, the lazy droop of his eyelids at variance with the bite in his voice, 'might have started off a little higher on the rungs than most; I'm not going to apologise for that. Any success I've achieved is due to damned hard work.'

And a razor-edged brain. He was being a little ingenuous, however, if he honestly believed that his concentrated authority and the sophistication that went with it—both of which owed a lot to his background—didn't have much to do with his rapid rise in his profession. As well, there were the contacts, both family and social.

The last word Tansy would apply to Leo Dacre was ingenuous.

She said 'OK, OK, I didn't mean that you were cheats and liars, and you know it. Just that advantage is not as unimportant as you think it is.'

'It's not so important, either,' he said, adding as he eased her from the crowd to their table, 'otherwise you, the daughter of a prostitute, brought up by foster-parents not exactly noted for their ambition, wouldn't have just finished a degree in one of the most esoteric aspects of our culture.'

He spoke dispassionately, yet Tansy shivered. Well, she had left herself open to that. No more confidences about her past!

He looked across the room, and immediately a waiter approached. Nice trick if you can manage it, Tansy decided. The equivalent of a triple somersault on the trapeze. The iron-clad confidence that intimated waiters into instant obedience was another legacy from his background.

Yet perhaps she was wrong. After the first glance it wasn't his clothes or his handsome face or his worldly charm that made him stand out; what impinged was his simple, forceful magnetism, the thousand subtle signals conveying that this man was a leader among men.

A bedrock of alpha male, she thought tartly, very nicely packaged in background and money. He was a winner. And she was no more immune to that very special brand of sorcery than any other person in the room. With a faint grimace she decided she'd like to see him in action in a courtroom.

No, she wouldn't. She didn't like men who hectored and bullied and pounced, men who used their considerable gifts to browbeat and entrap, which was what he did for a living.

'You have an intriguing line in expressions,' he said, having paid, and now ready to go.

She got to her feet, her smile twisting. 'Have I?'

'Very. One of these days I might be able to read them.'

As well as all his other advantages he had presence. A little ripple of interest like a small but detectable tide rip followed them across the room. It sent prickles across Tansy's skin, and starched her expression into rigidity.

A woman escorted by Leo Dacre would need to get accustomed to being stared at. In a purely reflexive gesture Tansy's hand wandered up to her hair. Fortunately before it got there she realised what she was doing and pulled it away. The stares were not for her. If anyone noticed her at all it would be to wonder what on earth she was doing with such a man.

The drive back to her flat was conducted in silence. Once more he came with her to her door, opened it, and checked the room. Living in such a confined space had made her very tidy, but if she was ever going to leave any underwear lying about tonight would be the occasion. However, a rapid glance reassured her.

Using formality to set him at a distance, she said, 'Thank you for a pleasant evening.'

'Thank you,' he said gravely.

It was difficult to see his face. The light from inside didn't quite reach it, and he loomed above her like some archetypal inhabitant of the night.

'I'll pick you up tomorrow at the same time,' he said.

'I'm singing at Arabella's——' she began.

'When do you finish?'

She bit her lip. 'Ten,' she said reluctantly. 'Too late to go out to dinner.'

'I'll meet you there.'

'Leo, it's not——'

'You made a promise.'

The steely note in his voice ruffled her composure. Stiffly, she said, 'All right,' as she turned to go inside.

'Tansy,' he said quietly, his deep voice lingering over the syllables of her name, 'you dance like a Bacchante. It's an image I'm not going to forget.'

Blindly she stepped into her room, shutting out his low laughter as she locked the door and put on the chain. A Bacchante indeed! He might just as well call her a drunkard as refer to the wildly dancing followers of the god of wine!

'It's my wretched *hair*, damn it,' she said weakly to the unresponsive door.

In spite of the deficiencies of her mirror she could see that her mouth was full and red, revealing secrets she didn't know she had, and her eyes were gleaming with a satisfaction that had something feline in it. Even her skin seemed burnished with a soft bloom of colour that stayed after she had removed the blusher.

Amazing what a handsome man did for your looks, she thought, using flippancy in an endeavour to calm her tumultuous thoughts as she climbed into bed. She should keep a tame one.

She had been lying there for some minutes when unease crawled through her. At first she thought it had something to do with the evening, but it turned out to be focused on Leo. And by asking herself questions she finally narrowed it down to the fact that she didn't believe him when he said he'd ask her where Rick was and then, no matter what her answer, leave her alone.

Leo had come to Wellington to find Rick, and he wouldn't go home without him. He was not a man accustomed to being thwarted.

Frowning, she turned her head fretfully on the pillow. The cold wind of the previous few days had died, and although it could hardly be called summery the weather was at last making some attempt to suit the season. But shivers were icing through her bloodstream.

It was useless to worry. Once she'd contacted the camp leader she'd know whether her gut-feeling was right, and that telling Leo where Rick was would be the worst thing she could do.

And if the leader disagreed, well, he could tell Rick, and Rick himself could contact his mother. That way he wouldn't feel he'd been dragged back from the camp by Leo.

She lay very still in the bed and went through the routine she'd evolved to calm herself down. It didn't help.

Eventually she went to sleep, worrying about Rick's mother. Although he had spoken of her with deep love, Tansy had formed an impression of a slightly neurotic woman, a woman who used her ailments to keep her family under control. However, there was nothing neurotic about cancer.

In the clear light of morning her fears of the night before seemed absurd.

And it was her birthday. Today she was twenty, out of her teens and able to legally go into a pub by herself, she thought as she flipped through the cards that arrived just after breakfast. Several from friends, one from a girl she'd become very close to at Mrs Tarawera's, another sent by a man on a scholarship in America.

And a letter from her landlord telling her that the house had been sold, and would she please be out of it by the end of March.

Fighting a sudden flare of panic, she clenched her hands. She'd find another place to live. Oh, it wouldn't be so convenient, but she'd find one.

Folding the letter back into the envelope, she stuffed it into a drawer, then arranged the cards on the windowsill, a little cheered by their bright pictures. None from her foster-parents. It was silly to be hurt—after all, she had rejected them—but she couldn't hide a tiny pang.

She always sent them birthday greetings. Still, they'd remember sooner or later; they always did.

Leaving her beret off in honour of the weather, she went out.

It was over-reacting, but as she slipped into a shop to ring the camp she had to stop herself from looking around nervously. She even stared through the window as she got through to the camp, just in case someone had been following her. Ridiculous!

When the camp leader, a tough, middle-aged man who pulled no punches, came on, she told him what was happening. After listening carefully, he thought for several moments, then said, 'No.'

'No what?'

'No, he's not ready to go. He's made great strides, I'm pleased with his progress, but if he goes now he's not going to come back, and that'll be a waste of a good human being.'

Tansy sighed. 'What about his mother?'

'I know it sounds callous, but either she's going to get better, in which case it would be silly for him to leave, or she's going to die. She doesn't need him for either. How sick is she?'

'I don't really know. She's had an op for cancer.'

'Well, if things get worse let me know. But leave it for as long as possible. Goodbye.'

Gnawing on her lip, Tansy replaced the receiver. It didn't raise her spirits to be vindicated.

Before walking out of the shop she assumed a studied composure that would probably fool no one. Guitar in one hand, she hitched her big cotton shirt with the other so that it lay more loosely across her breasts. 'If things get worse let me know'! She should have told the man she didn't really have anything to do with this sticky situation.

Well, it was her own fault; she had involved herself in Rick's life. Let that be a lesson to you, she told herself sardonically.

The interview with Professor Paxton was just as frustrating. There were no scholarships, no grants available.

'Don't give up,' he said at the end. 'I might find something. Anything is worth a try.' However forlorn the hope, his tone indicated.

Ironically, busking turned out to be quite profitable. Tansy didn't allow her morning to grind down her spirits for long. Somehow, even if she had to mortgage her future, she would find the money to finish her education.

In the meantime, she gave the Christmas shoppers everything she had, a selection of carols and seasonal songs and old favourites interspersed with some of the most popular of her own, and the money rolled in very nicely.

Just once, she thought as she packed up, she'd like to have enough money to be able to walk into a shop and buy whatever she wanted. A bookshop, say, or even a chemist. A nice thought, but it wasn't going to happen in the foreseeable future.

Last year she'd spent Christmas with a friend's family in Lower Hutt. They were darlings, and she'd been invited again, but a few months ago they'd moved to the Hawkes Bay and she couldn't afford the fare. It wouldn't be the first time she'd been alone at Christmas.

Later that evening at Arabella's everyone seemed in a festive mood, including Arabella herself, who whipped up such a frenzy of fun that Leo and Tansy didn't get away until midnight.

'I'm hoarse,' he grumbled.

Tansy sent him a mischievous glance. 'I'll give you some vocal exercises,' she promised. 'If you're going to make a habit of singing you should know how to look after your voice.'

He had a very pleasant baritone, completely un-
trained of course, but he knew how to use it effectively,
and she had been impressed by the number of songs he'd
known.

'I don't think I'll make a habit of it,' he said. 'Does
Arabella pay you extra when you organise a sing-song
like that?'

She smiled. 'No, and I didn't organise it, Arabella did.
I enjoy them.'

'She clucks over you like a hen with one chick.'

Tansy was a little light-headed. 'She never stops trying
to feed me up; she's convinced that if she serves me
enough free pasta I'm going to develop chubby cheeks
and dimples.'

He laughed. 'The mind boggles. She strikes me as
being fairly astute, so she must know that thorough-
breds don't fatten.'

'She's a determined woman,' Tansy told him
cheerfully.

He was driving her straight home, so presumably he
had given up any idea of persuading her to tell him where
Rick was. Just as well; she wasn't in any state to deal
with an argument. From beneath heavy eyelids she
looked out across the city to the hills that surrounded
it, lights to the very top revealing the desire of people
for a view, and their resistance to the winds. A yawn
shook her.

'I liked the man who sang "There's a Hole in My
Bucket",' Leo observed as they walked up the path to
her flat. 'Great style.'

She laughed softly. 'Truly impressive command of
dialect, too.'

At her door he said, 'I'd like to come in, if I may.
You did promise to listen to me.'

For a second she froze. She didn't want this; she didn't
want him in the flat, infiltrating it, stamping his presence

on it so that whenever she was home she would remember him there.

But she had agreed. Honour dictated her acquiescence.

'Yes, all right,' she said tonelessly.

Just as she'd suspected, he dwarfed the place. Waving him to the only chair, she sat on the side of the bed, miserably and angrily aware that he had probably never been in such surroundings before. The room she found comfortable and pleasant must appear squalid and depressing to him.

'I spoke to my stepmother's companion this evening,' he said without preamble, his eyes half closed so that all she could see beneath the dark lashes was a sliver of green fired by gold. 'Apparently Grace has convinced herself that if Ricky isn't home at Christmas it will be because he's dead.'

'I'm sorry,' Tansy muttered, trying to find some sort of path through this maze of emotions and motivations.

'Can you contact him?'

His eyes were fixed on the poster of the high Andes, but although the striking features revealed nothing she could feel his tension.

'No,' she said dully, hating herself for the lie.

'Are you sure?' he asked in a voice that was silkily menacing.

She said nothing.

'Will you at least tell me what he's doing?'

Her ribcage lifted as she took a deep breath. *'Don't tell Leo'*, Rick had pleaded. *'Whatever you do, Tansy, don't tell him where I am, what I'm doing. He doesn't believe in this sort of thing and he certainly doesn't believe I'm strong enough to do it on my own. He'd have me out of there in no time flat. Promise me you won't tell him. It's my only chance...'*

She said miserably, 'I can't, I'm sorry.'

'Can't? Or won't?'

She shook her head.

Before she had a chance to speak he said harshly, 'Tansy, his mother is ill; she wants Ricky, and perhaps she may need him to get better. If you want me to beg——'

'No!' She was being torn in two, her instincts inclining her one way, her knowledge that Rick was fighting the battle of his life another.

He needed to prove—to himself more than anyone else—that he was strong enough. Her conversation with the camp leader had made it fairly clear that if he were dragged home he'd go straight back to the situation he'd tried to escape.

Carefully, with an immense reluctance that she knew showed in her face, her tone, she muttered, 'Look, let me know how your stepmother is—when the tests come through. If she's—not well, I'll see what I can do.'

Leo looked at her with an unsparing contempt that stabbed through her like a sword, hard and unforgiving and lethal.

'Part of her problem,' he said evenly, 'is that she's afraid he's in trouble.'

Rick *was* in trouble, but he was dealing with it as best he could. Tansy said, 'He's not on the streets, if that's what you mean. He's not hungry. He's not dirty.'

'That tells me exactly nothing. Where the hell is he?'

She flinched, but managed to control the sudden flicker of fear. 'He's safe,' she said, her voice monotonous with the restraint she put on it. 'Leo, please go.'

'Mr Dacre to you.'

Her smile was acceptant, bitterly mocking. 'Very well, *Mr Dacre*, please go. I can't help you.'

'Tansy——'

'You're putting me into an impossible position,' she interrupted, low-voiced and intense. 'Damn you, Rick made me promise not to tell you where he is!'

'He had no right to extract a promise like that,' Leo returned, stone-faced. 'Just as you have no right to keep his whereabouts to yourself.'

She stared angrily into an implacable face. 'Why?'

'Because he's only a kid.'

'Rick is seventeen. Old enough to be making——'

'Old enough to have made an enormous hash of his life,' he said savagely. 'I can't work out whether you're deliberately stupid or the most gullible idiot I've ever come across.' Now he made no attempt to hide his frustrated fury. Spacing out the words so that they came like bullets, he said, 'He's a drug addict. Do you know that?'

Tansy's stomach lurched. 'Yes, of course I know. I didn't know whether you did, though.'

'No doubt,' he said mercilessly, 'you learned how to deal with drug addicts when you were a street kid.'

It was like being slapped in the face. Speaking carefully, she retorted, 'I've had dealings with addicts, yes.'

Mrs Tarawera had made no distinctions among those she took in.

Leo got to his feet and walked across to the window, staring out at the dreary side yard. One hand was pushed into his pocket. 'Then you must know that you can't believe a word an addict says. He needs professional help.'

'I don't know much about addicts of any sort, but I do know that it's no use trying to make people do things they're not ready for,' she said obstinately.

'So while we wait he could die of an overdose.'

'He won't.' She shook her head impatiently. 'Rick knows what a mess he's made of his life, and he's doing something about it.'

'Oh, for God's sake!' His clenched fist hit the windowsill with a jarring thud that made her gasp. 'He's a kid.'

'*You* think he's a kid. Why won't you let him grow up and be his own person, instead of making him feel totally inadequate because he's never going to be as big, and as macho, and as powerful as you are?'

He turned swiftly, startling her so that she flinched. As she watched, he reimposed control, calling on an awe-inspiring strength of will to fight the murderous rage her words had called forth.

'I might have known,' he said icily. 'It's my fault. I've been a convenient scapegoat for Rick's shortcomings all his life.'

'It's not your fault. You can't help it if he hero-worships you.' Tansy too had won a small battle with her temper. He had such formidable mastery of his own emotions that losing control of hers gave him an edge she couldn't afford. She went on, 'He's growing up. All right, so he's made mistakes. He knows that. If you come riding up like the cavalry and take over you'll just re-inforce his dependence, his failure to live up to some impossibly high Dacre standard. Let him handle this.'

'And if he doesn't?' he asked in a lethal tone. His green-gold eyes swept her face. 'Tell me, Tansy, so full of experience and good advice, if he struggles with his demons and can't overcome them, what happens then?'

It was her secret fear brought out into the open. She had lain awake these last few nights wondering whether she was being naïve and stupid in her conviction that left alone Rick would be able to cope.

Trying hard to hide the strain in her voice, she said, 'He's the only one who can help himself now. He's too old to be disciplined like a child. If this doesn't work, he's going to have to find another way. The only thing you can do for him is give him support. Basically, he's on his own.'

'Spoken like a true teenage runaway,' he sneered.

She looked at him steadily. 'That's what I was, and I survived.'

'Yes, but at what cost? Oh, you seem healthy enough, if a little hardened by it, but the scars don't need to show on the outside, do they? And you're tough and clever, whereas Rick is weak.'

'He's not as strong as you, perhaps, but he's not weak. He's been indulged, and he's easily led, but he knows that now.' She looked at him pleadingly, trying to make him understand. 'Look, he really wants to get out of the hole he's dug for himself, and that's more than half the battle. It's a battle he needs to fight for himself.'

'You'd know, I suppose. But how's he going to do it?'

Tansy remained silent, and he went on viciously, 'He's got no money, he can't earn enough to keep himself except by stealing or prostitution or dealing on his own account, and you say he'll cope! I warn you, Tansy, if anything happens to him, you'll suffer double for every last pain your intransigence causes.'

She thought he was going to say something else, but he got up and walked out without another word. He didn't even slam the door. It clicked almost silently behind him. Tansy jumped to her feet and locked it, then leaned her forehead against the solid wood, letting her breath out in a long, huffing sigh.

She had been in real danger there. She had tasted it, felt it like lightning in the air, sensed it in the swift response of her body, the sudden surge of adrenalin. That was why she felt so wrung-out now; she'd been unable to fight or flee, and the hormone rush had no place to go. Slowly she eased away from the door.

Thank heavens he was going back to Auckland tomorrow, because she wasn't going to be able to settle down until she was sure he was gone.

After yet another restless night she woke to a thunder of knocks on the door. Scrambling out of bed, she pulled her coat around her, her heartbeat shaking through her.

'Who is it?' she demanded, glowering.

'Leo.'

'Go away.'

He laughed. 'Open up, Tansy, or I'll kick the door in.'

She huddled deeper into her coat, wondering whether even Leo Dacre would do that. She should tell him to go to hell; slowly, reluctantly, she opened the chain and the door.

Leo stood there, charcoal hair glossed by the sun, his expression uncompromising, beautiful mouth held in a thin line that gave her fair warning.

'What do you want?' she asked, hiding apprehension with belligerence.

'Let me in.'

She shook her head but he put her to one side, his hands firm yet not painful, and came in anyway, turning to shut the door behind him.

'Get out of here right now,' she said very fast.

His eyes scanned her thick coat, her hair in its normal morning tangle like a wild aureole around her head, her face still flushed with sleep.

'Good morning, Tansy,' he said, smiling.

'What do you want?' She was holding her coat tight across her breasts, her long hands clenched so hard that the knuckles ached.

'You seem,' he said unhurriedly, 'to have the knack of tipping me on to the wrong foot. I didn't deal with things the way I should have last night. Why don't you go and wash your face and brush your hair and I'll make you a cup of coffee?'

'I haven't got any coffee,' she said aggressively.

'Tea, then.'

If he hadn't come so early she'd have been awake enough to realise that the door, though old, was too solid for him to kick in, but in her usual early morning stupor she hadn't been thinking straight.

More than anything she wanted to get into some clothes but there was no way she was going to take her bra and pants out of the chest of drawers with him watching. Without speaking she turned and strode into the bathroom, closing the door behind her with a definite thud.

By the time she came out again, hair combed, teeth cleaned and face washed, he had made tea and was sitting at the small bench drinking it. He should have looked incongruous in her room, dressed as he was in a darkly formal business suit, but he transcended the shabby surroundings. With a flash of resentment Tansy thought that he would look thoroughly at home wherever he was. Nothing could shake that inner assurance.

Whereas she was shivering inside, her whole being taut and stretched on the rack of her nerves. He made her feel inferior, and she hated it. Rick hadn't done that, although he had spoken of a life where people went away to boarding-school as a normal thing, where women rarely had careers, merely filling in time until they made good marriages, after which they ran their husbands' homes with style and efficiency.

Listening to Rick had been like reading a book; she knew there were people who lived like that, but she had never come across any before. And, she thought sullenly, she wouldn't care if she never saw another one.

Leo had looked up when she came through and smiled, yet she sensed a latent coldness in him that made her heart shake. She stopped herself from lifting her chin; it gave too much away, and, although men were not necessarily good at body language, Leo Dacre, with his courtroom training and keen intelligence, was an exception. She didn't want him to know that in some deeply hidden part of her soul she was afraid of him.

CHAPTER FOUR

'I'VE made some tea,' Leo said. 'I could only find some rather nasty peppermint stuff, but it's hot.'

'I don't like ordinary tea or coffee,' she snapped, sitting down as far away from him as the cramped little breakfast bar allowed. She picked up the mug he pushed towards her and drank the steaming liquid, thinking wryly that, if there was a time and a place for caffeine, now and here surely was it.

'What do you want?' she asked, when the silence stretched to uncomfortable limits.

'I lost my temper last night,' he said calmly. 'I don't know why, but you seem to be able to do that to me quite easily. Instead of flying off the handle I should have asked what I can do to persuade you to tell me where Ricky is.'

When she stared at him he directed one of his million-watt smiles at her and continued, 'I assume that if you didn't have to busk and play at Arabella's it would make your life a lot easier. So—I'll pay you for the information I want.'

Tansy put down her mug with a sharp little clink. The pattern on the faded, abraded benchtop danced suddenly in front of her eyes. Outside a car roared down the street, tyres squealing as it took the corner too fast.

On an indrawn breath she asked collectedly, 'Exactly what are you suggesting, *Mr Dacre*?'

'That I make sure you don't have to worry about money,' he said in a reasonable voice which chilled her more than open antagonism. 'And for heaven's sake, forget the insults. I was furious with you when I said that, and you know it.'

'Money,' she retorted contemptuously. 'In return for my betraying Rick? Thirty pieces of silver, I presume.'

He hid his anger better than she did, but it sizzled in his eyes, in his voice. 'Hardly so dramatic,' he said cuttingly. 'As for the betrayal bit—that depends entirely on where you stand, doesn't it?'

'I know exactly where I stand, and the answer is no,' she said harshly. 'Not even the prospect of lots of lovely Dacre money would persuade me to tell you how to get in touch with Rick. Get the hell out of here. You've tried intimidation and threats and seduction, and now that I've turned your money down there's nothing else you can use.'

He didn't answer, didn't move, but Tansy's gaze was dragged towards him by the inexorable force of his will.

Absolutely no emotion showed on the dark, determined face. The hooded eyes were slivers of pure colour, intense, feral. 'And that's your final word?' he asked smoothly.

She nodded, her face cold and proud and white beneath the riotous cloud of her hair.

'All right,' he said. In spite of the total lack of inflexion it sounded more like a curse than an agreement.

Even after the sound of his car had dwindled to nothing, Tansy couldn't stop the shudders that rose from somewhere inside her and shook her whole body.

She felt as though he had wreaked the greatest treachery on her. Searching for a reason, she realised she had hoped that in spite of everything he had—liked her a little. Her lips twisted in a sardonic smile. *Stupid*.

She was afraid. He hadn't lost his temper and shouted at her and crashed around as men did when they got angry. She could have coped with that. It was the formidable will that kept his temper under such brutal restraint that frightened her.

But at least he was gone. He'd go back to Auckland today, and, although he was furious with Tansy now, if his stepmother deteriorated he'd contact her again.

Please, she found herself saying, for everyone's sake let Mrs Dacre be all right.

She wanted nothing more than to crawl back into bed, pull the covers over her head and go to sleep until it was all over: her helpless, hopeless attraction to the man, the naïve feeling of betrayal and the quick, savage tug of fear.

But she had to work. She tipped the peppermint tea down the sink and washed and put away the mug. Ten minutes later she was dressed in a pair of jeans so old that they fitted her snugly, and another big shirt that skimmed her breasts and her hips to finish halfway down her thighs. After confining her hair in a baseball cap, she picked up her guitar case and set off for work.

All that morning she kept expecting him to turn up. It was ridiculous, but every time she looked down the street she thought she saw him. She was, she thought wearily, going mad.

So she concentrated on her singing. It was another good day. People enjoyed what she had to offer and tossed coins into her case with a liberality that spoke of the approaching holiday season. In the afternoon a group of Japanese tourists stopped to listen, applauding heartily. One girl, bolder than the rest, asked her for a song. Tansy sang her request, and they kept her busy for ten minutes or so, leaving her with a satisfying sum of money when they finally went.

By then it was after three, and Tansy was ready to go home. She slid her guitar strap from her shoulder and bent to scoop up the money from the case.

A couple of boys, fourteen or fifteen years old, and until then completely unthreatening, looked up and down the almost empty street, then at each other. She'd noticed them arrive half an hour before and had automatically kept an eye on them, but they'd done nothing to make her suspicious, merely sat talking and laughing and smoking.

Now, however, they had made up their minds and were closing in for what they clearly saw as easy money. Kicking her guitar case shut, Tansy put her instrument on to it and stepped over it towards them, holding the eyes of the one she guessed by his body language to be the leader.

'Which one of you is going to try?' she asked with a dangerous smile.

Obviously this was not the reaction they'd expected. Discomfited, they looked at each other, searching for reassurance. One giggled. 'Aw, shut up, bitch,' he said.

From behind them Leo Dacre said in a voice that froze Tansy's blood, 'On your way, both of you.'

But they had come too far to be able to back down without losing face. One looked over his shoulder and said offensively, 'F—— off,' and the other made a sudden lunge for Tansy.

She waited until he was close enough for her to thrust her strong musician's fingers into his eyes. Clawing at his face, he screamed and reeled back into his friend, who was being shaken like a rat by Leo.

Tansy stuck out her foot and her assailant tripped and fell. His friend landed on top of him, a wildly flailing mass of arms and legs.

'Let's go,' Leo said curtly.

Tansy hesitated, glancing up into a face that showed nothing of his emotions beyond a glittering intensity in his eyes. He wasn't even breathing heavily.

'We'd better make sure that one's all right,' she said worriedly. 'I got him in the eyes.'

'Tough. Get into the car!'

'My guitar——'

He scooped it up, closing the catches with quick, sure movements.

Tansy opened her mouth to object further when he slung an arm around her shoulder and carefully put her and the guitar into the vehicle that stood with its engine purring and its flashers on just down the street. Too taken aback to protest any further, Tansy sank into the comfortable seat and waited for him to get in.

Unfortunately her conscience pricked her. 'What about his eyes?' she said, turning around to look at the two who were just picking themselves up, mouthing curses and threats, but managing to look both smaller and sheepish at the same time.

'They'll be all right,' Leo said heartlessly. 'A jab isn't likely to blind him. With any luck he'll have a couple of corneal abrasions that'll keep him too busy for a while to attack women on the street.' He stopped at the lights. 'Put your seatbelt on.'

Obediently Tansy did up the seatbelt. 'I thought you were going back to Auckland,' she said uncertainly, dropping her purse on to the floor by her feet.

'I am, fairly soon. Do you get mugged often?'

'No.'

'Where did you learn to defend yourself?'

She thought briefly of the assortment of vagrants and streetkids who had lived at Mrs Tarawera's; between them they had known an infinite number of nasty methods of self-defence. 'I learned,' she said quietly.

'Very efficiently. I thought for a moment you'd let him come too close.'

'The thing is to keep them off balance. Neither of them thought they had anything to worry about, so they were careless.'

He said, 'They might not be so careless next time.'

Tansy repressed a shiver. Now that it was over she felt sick and shaky. 'Actually, there are not all that many times during the day when there's an opportunity like that. There are usually people in the street. It was their bad luck you happened to be driving past.'

'Wasn't it just?' He spoke grimly, yet she thought she heard a note of amusement in his words.

She looked up. While they were talking they'd been threading their way through the streets. Too busy fighting the bewildering complex of emotions engendered by seeing him after the early morning quarrel at the flat, Tansy hadn't really noticed.

But now, she realised incredulously, they were driving along the motorway. She demanded, 'Where are we going? This isn't the way home.'

'I thought we might have a drink together before I go.'

She stared suspiciously at him. 'Where, for heaven's sake? Porirua?' Her voice was heavy with sarcasm. 'Or perhaps Paraparaumu?' She gave the name of a distant suburb, and a seaside town an hour's drive from the city.

His mouth tugged upwards into a smile. 'Possibly,' he said blandly. 'Is there a place there where you can get a decent drink? Or perhaps we should just walk along the beach and talk.'

'What about?'

He passed a truck. 'I don't want to leave you the way I did this morning,' he said calmly.

'Oh.' Still warily sceptical, she tried to quench a tiny, unbidden warmth that flickered into life inside her.

'Did you have anything on this evening?'

'No,' she said slowly. 'But aren't you going back to Auckland?'

'Eventually.'

Shocked by the secret glow his words produced, she asked tentatively, 'Are we really going to Paraparaumu?'

'Yes. Tell me, do you agree with Freud when he said that music is a form of infantile escapism?'

Her indignant response to this open incitement kept her busy until she finally saw the signpost to Paraparaumu. When the car swept past the lights she asked, 'Where exactly are we going?'

He didn't look at her. 'Auckland.'

She said icily, 'So this is a kidnap. You, of all people, must realise how much you'll get for a sentence when the police catch up with you.'

His cynical smile screwed her temper up a notch. 'Tansy, the police aren't ever going to find out, and if you're unwise enough to tell them I'll simply say that you're trying to get back at me for breaking up with you.'

'They wouldn't believe that!'

He laughed softly. 'Of course they would.'

She stared at an implacable profile, sharply etched against the afternoon sky, and realised that he was almost certainly right. When it came to the word of a man like Leo Dacre, she'd be disbelieved.

'After all,' he went on in the same infuriatingly reasonable tone, 'you got in with me quite happily; there were people about who saw you, who can testify that you weren't flung into the car and carried off. And as we've been seen around town together, there are plenty of others who will testify that we are—how can I put this delicately, I wonder?'

'There is no way you *can* put it,' she said fiercely, because anger disguised the deep, shattering anguish that clawed through her. 'Damn you, you set me up!'

'I don't make a habit of laying myself open to counter-attacks,' he said with a cool self-possession that infuriated her even as it sent a pang of primitive fear jabbing her stomach. He looked sideways at her, his eyes crystalline and dispassionate. 'I'm a careful person,' he said. 'Remember that, Tansy, and we'll get along very well.'

Over the years she had learned to control her temper, but at this blatant piece of provocation she came perilously close to erupting into a real kicking and screaming tantrum. Clinging to her composure, she said, 'I'll be missed.'

'No, you won't. I told the couple upstairs that you were coming away with me for Christmas, so if anyone does come sniffing about they'll be able to tell them you're fine.'

Tansy ground her teeth together. The tentative beginnings of liking, the pleasure she'd reluctantly found in his company, had been in response to a cold-blooded campaign. She should have known that a man like Leo Dacre had no interest in a woman like her. Instead she had let unformed, barely recognisable needs fool her usual common sense into some kind of sickly hope.

Almost choking on the words she demanded, 'Why are we going to Auckland?'

'I want you to meet Grace.'

She was speechless then, because although she hadn't been able to see beyond the handsome façade, he understood her only too well. It was much easier to refuse something long-distance than to say a direct no to a woman who might be very ill.

'One of these days,' she said evenly, 'I'm going to make you pay for this.'

He smiled. 'How?'

'I don't know yet, but I'll find a way.'

Until that moment she'd considered revenge a waste of time. She was beginning to see why people spent their lives planning it.

From then on while the car ate up the miles she refused to speak. How dared he take so little account of her that he thought he could get away with this! And how utterly stupid of her to feel as though he had broken some unspoken trust.

At Otaki she tried to get out at the traffic-lights, but of course he'd locked her door, and by the time she'd realised this the lights had changed and the big car drew away.

He didn't say anything, but the straight line of his mouth was tucked up slightly in amusement. Boiling with rage and torment, Tansy had to sit on her hands to keep them from hitting him. The next opportunity I get, she thought angrily, however distant rescue seems, I'll yell and scream and bang on the door. Someone will notice.

But there was no next time. The car swept smoothly through farmland and small country towns, heading north into the less settled reaches of the North Island. By the time dusk approached they had reached the central plateau, a barren sweep of land dominated by three big volcanoes. Ahead lay Taupo, the huge lake left when, in one of the biggest explosions of all time, another volcanic vent had covered almost half the North Island with ejecta two thousand years ago.

As they drove along the desert road the summer sun turned the snows of Ruapehu crimson, tipped conical Ngauruhoe lilac, and picked out ultramarine shadows on the white peak of Tongariro. At Turangi Leo took the left-hand road and headed up the western side of Lake Taupo. Tansy's stomach rumbled.

'Almost there,' he said cheerfully.

She stared obstinately through the side-window. Clearly they weren't going to drive through the night. If they stopped somewhere she could ring the police.

And then see how he'd wriggle out of that, she thought viciously. Because he was Leo Dacre they might find it hard to believe, but they'd have to listen to her if she laid a formal complaint.

Sooner or later he had to learn that there were limits to his power and influence. Lost in vengeful thoughts, she realised with a jolt that it was almost dark, and that he was turning the nose of the car down a secondary road. After some time they left that for a track that needed urgent repairs.

'There's a fishing cabin down here,' he told her, 'that belongs to friends of mine. We'll spend the night there.'

He waited. When she said nothing he resumed, 'There's no one about. No one at all. And no telephone, I'm afraid.'

Although she didn't respond her intense chagrin probably showed. Oh, well, she thought grimly, there'd be a chance tomorrow. All she had to do was keep her wits about her so that when the opportunity appeared she recognised it and took it.

Small and very basic, the fishing cabin crouched behind a narrow pumice beach; to one side was the mouth of a stream that chattered down from the hills behind. Huge bluffs rose like the dark walls of hell to the north, but to the south lower hills and bush stretched away, the occasional plume of steam reminding Tansy of the area's volcanic origins.

There was no other cabin, no boat in sight, no sound but the gentle grinding of the pumice pebbles against each other and the noise of the little creek, nothing to see but the calm waters of Lake Taupo stretching over thirty kilometres to the hazy distant shore, rendered gold by the last rays of the sun into an enchanted country.

'You might as well stop sulking,' Leo said casually as he got out. 'There's no one to impress, and I promise I won't hold it against you if you decide to talk.'

Tansy sat mutely in the car, staring fixedly through the windscreen.

'Passive resistance,' he observed thoughtfully, coming around to her side of the car. 'Yes, probably as good a way as any to deal with the situation.'

Without hesitation he reached across, clicked free her seatbelt, and lifted her from the seat. Humiliated, Tansy stiffened even further, forcibly blocking the faithless senses that awoke at the scent of his body, warm and slightly musky and very masculine, and the strength of the arms that held her. He strode across the coarse grass as gracefully as though he habitually carried women about, the smooth, powerful movements of his body setting up an elemental reaction deep inside her.

'If you want me to put you down,' he said, juggling her slight weight with insulting ease while he inserted a key into the lock, 'you only have to ask.'

Tansy looked up. He smiled, but there was an unsparing detachment in the green-gold eyes that warned her he meant it.

Still, he couldn't go on carrying her around all night. She was damned if she was going to ask him for anything. Refusing to give him the small surrender, she stared mutinously back.

'When I realised that I'd have to make you see with your own eyes just what your refusal to tell us where Ricky is was doing to Grace, I knew you'd never come willingly. Which left me with only one alternative,' he said meditatively, pushing the door open to reveal a living-room that had a kitchen off one end, and a couple of doors off the other.

He set her down on her feet and smiled, green eyes gleaming suddenly. He didn't let her go.

Very much aware of her size and his, of the faint, subliminal signals she was receiving from him, she said harshly, 'Does your family know you're certifiable?'

His smile deepened. 'You've such a pretty mouth,' he said, his voice caressing as his eyes lingered on her lips. 'It's a pity you keep it under such fierce control, like caging a flower.' He paused. 'Come with me to Auckland, Tansy. See what you're doing to Grace. You owe her that, at least.'

Promises extracted under duress didn't count. And at that moment Tansy was fighting an insidious traitor deep inside, a flicker of response that would grow to a full-blown flame if she let it.

'All right,' she said before she had time to feel shame, finishing briskly, 'Now will you let me go?'

'Certainly.' He spread his arms wide.

Tansy stepped back with such haste that she stumbled. Swiftly he caught her, but let her go free as soon as she'd regained her balance.

'Where's the bathroom?' she muttered, desperate to get away.

'The left-hand door. Straight through the bedroom.'

The bedroom contained a large double bed, and was as basic as the rest of the house. In the bathroom Tansy looked at the window, muttering beneath her breath as she saw that like the one in the bedroom it had a deadlock, and of course there was no sign of a key. To get out she'd have to shatter the glass.

But first she'd have to knock Leo unconscious. And even if she managed that and got free she'd need to steal the car, because the main road lay at least twenty kilometres away. Always providing, of course, that Leo wasn't disabling it right now. Which meant she'd better bank on walking out to the main road.

Why, she wondered angrily as she washed her hands, didn't he carry a cellphone in his car like all other yuppies?

A thump from the living-room interrupted her thoughts. Swiftly, before he had a chance to come and catch her, she looked around, searching for something she could use to knock him out with. Unfortunately, the room was completely devoid of anything that looked remotely like a weapon. No vases, not even a lamp. Subduing the squeamishness that assailed her at the thought of hitting anyone, she gave the bedside table a tentative tug, but let it go when she realised it was part of the bedhead.

She didn't ask herself why it was so important that she get away, but even though she knew he wouldn't hurt her the need to escape was like a fire inside her, lighting a rashness that had never been there before.

There had to be some way of getting out. During the night he'd sleep, and unless he had handcuffs in the car that was likely to be her only chance. And surely in the kitchen there was a frying-pan or something she could use to hit him with? Her stomach lurched, but she set her mouth stubbornly.

He wasn't going to get away with this. He had to be shown that even if he was Leo Dacre he couldn't ride roughshod over the peasants. It made them testy.

After a last glance around the room she straightened her shoulders and went back through the door.

Leo was just finishing the carving of a cold roast chicken. He put the dish on the bench beside two dinner plates and a couple of plastic bowls. One had potato salad in it, and there was something fresh and crisp and green in the second. Next to the kettle were two mugs. The table had been covered with a cloth and two places set. Tomatoes in another bowl gleamed redly by salt and pepper shakers.

All very domestic, Tansy thought dourly, her gaze skimming the food on its way to the door. Disappointment weighed her down when she saw that it was deadlocked. The key, of course, was nowhere to be seen.

He'd noticed that compulsive glance, but he said nothing more than, 'Here, have something to eat. I hope it tastes as good as it smells.'

Although fury and fear had ruined her appetite, she knew she needed to keep her strength up, so she forced the food down. He'd even organised herbal tea for her. Outside night fell smoothly, wrapping them in darkness. No noise broke the immense silence. It frightened her, yet a latent wildness in her responded to the immeasurable tranquillity.

Suddenly a phrase of music that had been hovering for days around the edge of her mind crystallised into being. Her eyes darted around the comfortable room.

'The door's locked,' Leo said sharply.

'I need some paper,' she said, frantic to get it down before it disappeared into limbo.

Without comment Leo yanked a blank scribble pad from his briefcase and handed it over. Afterwards she'd be surprised that she could write in front of this man, but at the time she was too lost in delight to realise.

It came easily, the melody flowing from the bottomless wells of her mind, the simple theme, and a subsequent intricate reworking of it, counterpoint and harmony, dissonance, finishing with a slow and dramatic finale.

When it was done, she lifted her head, shaking with tiredness, the euphoria draining away to a dull lassitude. It was the best thing she'd ever done, and she knew it. Strange that it should happen now, and in this man's company...

'Bed,' Leo said laconically, apparently not in the least surprised or even interested.

In some ways, she thought wearily, he was oddly restful. Perhaps it was the aftermath of working that made her so apathetic, but it wasn't until she reached the doorway that she realised where they were heading, and stopped. 'Where are you sleeping?' she demanded.

'In there,' he said promptly, the amused note in his voice failing to hide the uncompromising undertone.

'I am not sleeping with you.'

His hand came up and fastened around the back of her neck. Although the fingers rested gently on her skin, a shiver of apprehension coursed down her spine. 'You're going to do exactly what you're told,' he said without heat. 'I'm not going to take advantage of the situation, I give you my word.'

Tansy opened her mouth but before her furious objections could tumble free he continued quietly, 'If you're not reasonable about this, I'll tie you up. You'll still sleep with me, but it will be extremely uncomfortable.'

He wouldn't do it. He wouldn't dare. She turned her head and met eyes that were narrowed and blazing with a cold fire, merciless and inexorable.

Her own eyes widened. Hastily she looked away.

'Be sensible,' he said, quite calmly yet without any yielding. 'Go and have your shower.'

Numbly, she showered. She had no change of clothes so she had to put back on the ones she'd taken off. Wrinkling her nose, she used the wrapped toothbrush and small new tube of toothpaste.

Then she went back into the bedroom. 'I've finished,' she said stonily.

'I won't be long.' He looked at her averted face. 'The door is locked, and so are all the windows. If you try to break one I'll be out before you have a chance to clear the broken glass away.'

He left the door open, too. Tansy waited until the shower was full on, then went around the room, testing the windows, testing the door. They remained obdurately closed. The hiss of the shower made her wonder whether she could smash the window without him hearing, but she doubted it. Besides, there was still nothing in the room that would serve to break the glass.

Moving soundlessly, she opened the wardrobe door. By now she wasn't expecting any help, and sure enough, it was empty, except for a hat on the shelf with what she supposed were fishing flies stuck in the band. Frustrated and angry, she thumped the wall with her fist.

Instantly, the shower stopped. Within seconds Leo stood in the doorway. He hadn't bothered to drag a towel around him, and the sight of his naked body sent Tansy's mind into shock and stopped her heartbeat for a long, tense moment.

Glistening with water, every contour as glossily outlined as those on the oiled bodybuilders on the covers of muscle magazines, Leo Dacre was superbly made, with none of the opulent exhibitionism of those men. Coppery skin spread sleek and shining across torso and broad shoulders; a pattern of hair, old as time, scrolled over his chest, and arrowed down...

Hastily Tansy turned her face away, hating the colour that rioted through her skin, hating him for being so casual about nudity that he could appear in front of a stranger without any sign of embarrassment. How many other women had seen him like this? Hundreds, if his total lack of modesty was any indication.

His eyes took in her clenched fist, her angry face. Saying casually, 'You'll only hurt yourself if you do that sort of thing,' he turned away.

Tansy shut her eyes tight, waiting until a sneaked look from beneath flickering lashes revealed an empty doorway.

Her legs felt strangely boneless, and an odd heat curled though her body, sapping her strength in a lazy, heated languor. Her brain seemed unable to do anything but linger on his image as though it was burnt into her cells.

It was the first time in her life she had seen a naked man, and she couldn't help the overwhelmed awe that had rocketed through her. She had heard men described as beautiful, had admired paintings and statues and photographs, but nothing had made such an impact as Leo.

'All right,' he said, emerging. 'You can open your eyes.'

She turned a glittering gaze on him. He had on a pair of boxer shorts and nothing else, and, to her horror, she felt once again that scorching tide through her skin.

His brows shot up. 'You're very prudish,' he said, mockery like a seam of chocolate through his tone. 'I'll turn my back while you take off your clothes.'

A gathering darkness coalesced inside her. She said tonelessly, 'If you rape me I'll make it as hard for you as I can, and once I'm free, so help me, I'll come after you.'

Once more his brows lifted. He looked at her for a moment, his expression arrested, as though she wasn't reacting in the way he expected. Then those broad, gleaming shoulders moved in a slight shrug. 'I'm not going to touch you,' he said impatiently. 'I've already told you that.'

'You expect me to believe you?'

'Quite frankly, I don't care whether you do or not. I'm quite capable of restraining my animal lust.' He waited, then said with an impatience that hurt her obscurely, 'Oh, if it makes you feel any better, keep your jeans on, but that shirt comes off.'

Colder than she had ever been, she unbuttoned it. He didn't watch, just stood there, big and inflexible and dominating, humiliating her. Hatred for him surged like a black tide through every cell in her body. How on earth could she have thought she was attracted to him?

Yet, absurdly, she was angry with herself for wearing a bra that should have been replaced at least a month before.

'Give me the shirt,' he said, obviously totally unmoved.

She flung it on the floor, got in between the sheets and lay facing the edge of the bed with her eyes closed, lashes lowered over crimson cheeks, her straight back stiff with outrage. After a few seconds he got in beside her.

'I'm a light sleeper,' he said, sounding bored, 'so I'll know the minute you stir.'

'I'm not going to——'

'Look, just stop arguing, will you? Go to sleep.'

In a shaking voice she said, 'I will never forgive you for this.'

'Tell me where Ricky is and I'll take you back now.'

She folded her lips obstinately.

'Goodnight, Tansy,' he said collectedly, and to her fury and despair went to sleep.

Normally she tended to lie and stare at the ceiling for half an hour or so before she finally slept. For some unexplained reason this night she went to sleep immediately, but not before she had impressed on her mind that she wanted to wake at one in the morning.

She had no idea whether it really worked, but when she did wake it was dark, without any sign of approaching dawn, and Leo Dacre was still sleeping quietly.

Unfortunately, she realised with an alarm close to panic, he was sleeping with his arms around her and she was snuggled up against his warmth as though they slept like this every night. Cheek pressed to the hard plane of his chest, she could hear his heart beating slowly and steadily, and her nostrils were filled with his particular male scent, faint but extremely potent.

Even worse, she woke to a languid, replete contentment, so consuming that it seemed to permeate her bones. It was as big a betrayal as the fact that she had been able to write in front of him.

Awake or asleep, he wasn't unmoved by her closeness, either. The hard pressure against her hip stirred her unbearably.

Fear washed over her. The unbridled longings of her body, disturbing and destructive, were far more of a danger to her than his cavalier abduction—she could understand why he had done that, even if she didn't condone it.

But she certainly didn't understand why her instincts had been burned away by this honeyed fire. She should be cowering on the edge of the bed, not snuggling into the man as though the only place on earth she wanted to be was in the sweet imprisonment of his arms.

Holding her breath, she began to ease away. Instantly his arms tightened, bringing her back against him.

'No,' he said indistinctly.

Tansy froze. Was he awake?

She risked a glance, but couldn't see anything of his face. Quite possibly, she thought with a sudden, fierce ache, he spent most nights with a woman, so this was nothing unusual for him.

Setting her jaw, she rolled over as though she too were sound asleep, and arranged herself facing the edge of the bed. This time he didn't make any attempt to keep her in his arms. Immensely relieved, she lay very still. Surely her heart pounding in her breast was enough to wake the dead! She tried to regulate her breathing, but far from calming her it had the opposite effect. When he muttered something and turned over, panic kicked evilly in her stomach.

However, after a moment, his breathing resumed its deep, even tenor. So he was still asleep.

Tansy waited for her pulses to slow down, the churning turmoil in her stomach to ease. Somehow it was difficult to remember exactly why she had to get out of this warm bed and grope her way outside into the darkness. After all, what harm could it do to go with him to Auckland, say no to his stepmother and leave?

My God, she thought, I'm making excuses to stay here!

Slowly she eased herself from the bed, and searched for her shirt, then, abandoning it, tiptoed to the bathroom and wrapped a towel around her bra. She was going to be as warm as she possibly could be while plodding down that road.

Leo slept serenely on while she made her way across the bedroom to the door. Cautiously, hardly daring to breathe, she tried the handle. It didn't move. Frustration almost boiled over. She pressed her fingers against her mouth, holding back the fury and the despair.

All right, so the door was still locked. She'd expected that. Where would he put the keys? Her eyes wandered across to the wardrobe.

No, too easy. But she tried the pockets of his trousers and shirt, biting back a curse at their emptiness.

By now her eyes were attuned to the darkness; she could see the long hump on the bed that was Leo, the white splash of the sheet across his shoulder and chest. The safest place to hide anything would be between the mattress and the base of his side of the bed. She hadn't noticed him put anything there, but then, she'd been lying with her back to him.

He hadn't stirred and his breathing hadn't altered a bit, so, in spite of his boast he was no light sleeper. Tansy swallowed, and licked parched lips.

It mightn't work, but at least she would have tried. No, she thought starkly, creeping softly as a whisper across the room, trying didn't count. She'd damned well get those keys out, and she'd open the door, and she'd walk out of the cabin. And then he'd be the one to be helpless, because the first thing she'd do was go to the police.

She was at the foot of the bed when he flung out an arm, and she thought her heart might burst the constraints of her flesh and explode. She froze, eyes huge and strained. Forcing air into her lungs, she watched his inert form, striving to hear above the sound of her heart any change in his breathing.

Eventually, when one foot got pins and needles, she crept forward. Blocking out her queasy apprehension with memories of the humiliation he had forced on her, she set her teeth and bent down, hardly daring to breathe as her slim fingers slid slowly beneath the mattress.

CHAPTER FIVE

'YOU haven't a hope,' he said, his voice husky with sleep but the hand that fastened around her wrist moved as swiftly and surely as a snake striking prey.

Sheer terror fountained through her in an icy flood, scrambling her brains, a bitter corrosion in her mouth.

He laughed without amusement. 'Get back into bed,' he said, and pulled her between the sheets.

Tansy arrived all in a rush against him, just as she'd been when she first woke, but this time he was wide awake with anger vibrating through him.

'Let me go,' she panted, pushing against his shoulders.

'Like hell,' he said between his teeth, his hands tightening around her back.

As Tansy fought viciously, his male flesh quickened and rose against her. That was bad enough. But infinitely worse was the urgent incandescence of her primitive, untrammelled response, burning like an elemental enchantment through her. She brought her knee up, but couldn't move quickly enough, and in an instant he was lying across her, strong legs holding hers pinned, his chest crushing her into the mattress, his forearm across her throat.

Almost before she had formulated the thought her small, serviceable fists jarred into his ribs on both sides of his torso, but although he flinched the steely arm across her throat pressed even further down, cutting off her wind.

As she brought her hands up ready to tear at his eyes, he commanded roughly, 'Tansy, no! I'm not going to hurt you!'

His voice echoed through the frantic thunder of her heart. The scent of her own fear was acrid in her nostrils, yet at some instinctual level his words convinced her.

Thinly she croaked, 'Let me go.'

The wicked pressure lifted. 'Are you all right?' he demanded.

'Yes.'

Breathing heavily, he said, 'I'm sorry. I shouldn't have reacted like that, but of all the stupid, idiotic things to do——! I could have hurt you quite badly, you little fool.'

'I may be a fool,' she returned fiercely, 'but I'm not a kidnapper. I don't force people to do what I want. I can handle a refusal without imposing my will on others.'

'Oddly enough, so can I, normally,' he said with barely curbed anger. 'But this is different.'

'Oh, of course it is! Get off me, damn you.'

He rolled over on to his side. 'Turn over.'

'What?'

'Tansy, turn over, now.' His voice was harsh and peremptory. 'Otherwise I'll take it that you aren't averse to what's going to happen in a very short time if you stay like that.'

Gulping, she whipped around and presented her back to him in one jerky movement.

'Good,' he said and tucked her spoon-fashion into him, one arm beneath her neck, the other folded firmly around her waist. 'Now, get back to sleep. We've got five hours before we need to get up.'

Tansy lay stiff and tense, her whole body screaming danger. Because even though Leo was completely despicable, some voluptuous, unsuspected weakness in her preened. Damn, she thought. Damn, damn, *damn*! I don't like him, I don't trust him an inch, I certainly don't love him, but I want him. Of all the men in the world, I had to choose Leo Dacre.

Trying not to feel the steady lift and fall of his chest, trying to repress the unbidden reaction of her body, trying to ignore the fact that he was still aroused, she stared straight ahead while her brain replayed the events of a few minutes ago.

She hadn't had a chance. Oh, she'd probably have been able to damage him—she knew tricks he might have no defences against—but he'd moved so fast, like a powerful animal defending itself, and he'd known exactly how much pressure he could exert before he cut off her breath completely. Surely sophisticated barristers didn't learn things like that at law school?

And he had let her go. Although he had been angry, he had controlled it almost immediately. Just as he'd controlled his reaction to her body.

She might despise him, but she recognised the first stirrings of a reluctant, antagonistic respect. Emotions and recollections swirled through her foggy brain until eventually she fell asleep.

It was light when she woke, barely dawn, but she was alone in the bed, for which she was devoutly thankful. Last night it had been too easy to forget that Leo thought so little of her that he'd stolen her away from her own life to suit his own purposes.

When her foster-family and the social worker assumed they knew better than she did what was good for her, Tansy had fled; she had worked and scrimped and saved and gone without food and clothing and the pretty things she'd have loved because she refused to be anything other than her own woman.

At least then everyone had thought they were doing what was best for her. Leo Dacre had no such excuse. However good his reason, she didn't believe that he normally kidnapped people, so it was even more humiliating that he thought he could get away with doing it to her.

Although probably not many people refused to do what he wanted. And she was dangerously vulnerable to the glittering, potent sexuality that had enmeshed her in its elemental sorcery the night before.

The sound of the opening door made her squirm hastily beneath the covers.

'Good morning,' Leo said crisply. 'Time to get up.'

He carried a cup of peppermint tea which he put on the bedside table, apparently not in the least thrown by having a woman in his bed.

Well, no. You didn't get that air of expertise without some practice!

Tansy stared mutinously at him.

'Back to passive resistance?' He sounded amused, his smoothly handsome face barely concealing a lurking mockery that infuriated her. 'You know, when you're asleep that firm, disciplined mouth relaxes into softness, and you look very young and innocent.'

She hated the thought of him seeing her asleep, hated it with a passion that shocked her. His conversational tone didn't fool her a bit. He didn't consider her at all innocent. As his gaze drifted down across the sheet she realised he was remembering what it had felt like to hold her so close during the night. Allied to the casual mention of how she looked asleep it was a subtle power play, one she had no defence against.

No defence but her silent defiance. And although she stared at him with blazing, hostile eyes, will-power didn't stop the blood from staining her skin.

He smiled and said deliberately, 'I wonder if you realise just what a challenge those tiger eyes are, tawny and fierce and provocative? They flash like topazes, and make me wonder whether you would burn as ardently in my arms.'

Even more hectic colour licked along her cheekbones, but she held his gaze, refusing to back down.

'Drink up,' he commanded coolly as he left the room. 'We leave in half an hour.'

Shaken yet fuming, Tansy drank the hot liquid and hurried into the shower. She fancied she could smell traces of his male scent on her skin, and she was determined to scour it away, but first she washed and wrung out her bra and pants. As she twisted the towel around them she wondered what she was going to do about clothes. The bra might just dry in time, but her pants were cotton; apart from being horridly uncomfortable, they were going to show in damp patches through her jeans.

Another thing to mark up against Leo's name. Imagining several very satisfactory ways of making him suffer, she slammed into the shower. Whoever fished here took their comfort very seriously; the shower was housed in a separate little room, with its own door, and was warm and light and equipped with the latest in technology. The head itself almost needed a licence to work; she had only ever seen anything like it in advertisments.

People who could afford to spend such money on a holiday home had nothing in common with most New Zealanders; certainly not with her.

When she emerged, the jeans and shirt, even her bra and pants, were gone. For a moment she stared through the door, her body icy.

Don't over-react, she scolded, trying to steady the sudden acceleration of her pulses. If he'd wanted to rape her he'd have done it last night, not waited until morning. Perhaps he'd put the underwear in a dryer somewhere. She wrapped herself in a towel, firmed her mouth and went through into the bedroom.

Her clothes were nowhere in sight. Instead, in plain view on the stripped bed were jeans—the right size—and a T-shirt in a bright terracotta shade that would clash violently with her hair. Brand new bikini pants and a soft bra-top were still in their packets.

A mixture of fury and wistfulness vied for power within her. She hated the thought of him touching her clothes; to wear things he had bought for her would put her in the same position as the prostitute he thought she'd been. Pride dictated that she refuse them, but pride didn't tell her how to get her own clothes back.

And it had been so long since she had bought anything new for herself except for underwear—and never such pretty things as these.

Biting her lip, she got into the pants and bra-top—how had he managed to guess so accurately the size of her breasts when she kept them hidden as much as possible?—and pulled on the stiff new jeans and the bright T-shirt. Reducing her hair to order back in the bathroom, she realised that the T-shirt didn't clash with her obnoxiously ginger locks; if anything the vibrant colour toned them down. And instead of its normal sallow colouring, her skin was transformed by the T-shirt into ivory.

So, add to Leo's manifold sins the fact that he knew better than she did what colours suited her. Of course, when everything you owned came from the charity shop, you bought for size and the wear left in the garment, and accepted the colours they came in with resignation. But even if she'd been buying new clothes, she'd never have considered terracotta!

Eventually she stuffed her feet into her shoes, angled her chin pugnaciously, and walked through into the living area of the cabin.

Leo was in the kitchen making toast. He saw her swift glance at the locked door, and said evenly, 'Give up, Tansy. It will make things much easier for you.'

'For you, you mean,' she said in a tart voice. 'Thank you for the clothes.'

Scooping up the toast he put the two pieces into the rack and pushed it across the breakfast bar. 'Eat up,' he said. 'I wonder why it seems to me that you find my buying you clothes even more offensive than my kidnapping you.'

'Because you're intuitive?' She didn't even try to hide the sarcasm in her tone.

He lifted straight, dark brows and looked at her consideringly. 'Think of this as a holiday. You'll be able to ease off on the stress and when you go back to Wellington you'll be a new woman.'

When she glared at him, he smiled with a hard irony that made her bristle and almost broke her resolution to remain silent and controlled. Biting back the tumbling words, she sat down, her expression coldly determined.

Not hungry, she nevertheless ate two pieces of toast and drank the orange juice he poured for her. To her relief he ate his much larger meal in silence. Afterwards, in a parody of togetherness, they cleaned up; she washed the dishes and he dried and put them away.

The sun beamed down on the blue, serene lake, glinting in golden patinas wherever its rays caught the smooth surface. In the fresh morning light the hills glowed a myriad shades of green, wispy plumes of steam from fumeroles adding an unearthly air to the familiar textures of bush. No sound broke the silence.

'One of my favourite places,' Leo remarked. 'The fishing's good, too. I caught my first rainbow trout just off here.'

'Is it stuffed and mounted in your study?' she asked dulcetly.

'I don't have a study, I have an office. And no, of course it's not. We ate it. I don't believe in killing anything I'm not prepared to eat, unless it's an ecological disaster like the possum and the rat.'

'It's nice to know you have some morals,' Tansy said, even more sweetly.

Lazy humour lit his eyes. 'You have a nasty tongue. Ah, well, I suppose you're entitled to be angry with me.'

'Angry?' she said lightly. 'Don't be so stupid. I'm not angry with you; I'm bloody furious!'

They reached Auckland at midday. Before then, hoping for a chance to get away, Tansy demanded they stop at a restroom, but he foiled her there, too, taking her to a unisex one that had bars on the window, and waiting outside until she emerged. He couldn't possibly have organised it so no one would be around, but that was how it happened.

She resumed her mulish demeanour. Not that it seemed to impress him at all. Apparently amused rather than chastened by her obstinate lack of co-operation, he dropped an occasional comment into the frigid silence.

Towards the Bombay Hills he asked unexpectedly, 'Did Ricky tell you he'd been extremely sick when he was a baby?'

Before she had time to realise what she was doing she nodded.

'You may think Grace is too possessive, but she went through hell, especially when they discovered that it was a hereditary condition she'd passed on to him.'

Tansy folded her lips tightly.

'I don't think she's ever really recovered,' Leo went on, apparently idly. 'She's always blamed herself for everything that's gone wrong in his life. She's fiercely maternal, and my father dying so young left her with no one else but Ricky as the recipient of all that emotion. She should have had a family of five or six.'

'She could have loved you,' Tansy snapped, then coloured angrily and looked out of the side window.

His smile sounded in his voice. 'She did love me. She was the best sort of stepmother, loving and kind and understanding enough to let me grow up and make my own mistakes. Yes, I can see from the set of your shoulders that you think she should do the same for Rick, but circumstances were different—I had rude good health. I don't think she's able to look at Ricky even now without superimposing an image of the child who damned near died in her arms more times than I care to remember.'

Tansy kept her face turned away.

'Can't you see why she's so worried?' he said. 'Any mother would be if her child had run away, but with Grace it's like losing him to death again, especially as she's terrified he's in deep trouble.'

Oh, yes, Tansy could see, but she had to weigh Grace Dacre's welfare against Rick's, and, unfortunately for his mother, Rick's won out.

By keeping her attention on the world flashing by, she hoped to drown out the guilt Leo's words had caused, and to a certain extent she succeeded. She'd forgotten how hot an Auckland summer's day could be. Even in the luxurious car the humidity was trying, so she was more than grateful for the air-conditioning, although she couldn't resist pointing out righteously that by using it he was adding to the hole in the ozone layer.

'Turn it off if you want to,' Leo said.

She did, but then had to lower the window to cool the rapidly heating interior, and that meant breathing in damp, warm air heavily laced with petrol fumes. Casting him a resentful glance, she realised with chagrin that the heat didn't seem to worry him. The autocratic profile and smooth, faintly coppery skin showed no shine of dampness, whereas a trickle of sweat was already making its way down the centre of her back.

She also felt a stirring in her inner regions. Those moments spent in his arms, and her subsequent realisation that she wanted him, had affected her at some basic, cellular level. Before then she had been able to look at him with little more than the superficial admiration of any woman for a handsome, dynamic man, but now other emotions were mixed in with the straightforward appreciation of the eyes.

Reluctant though she was to admit it, he had touched a previously inviolate part of her, and she was never again going to be the same. He'd made her acutely aware of him, attuned to him in a way that wasn't logical because it had nothing to do with her brain.

It stung that it should be this man, who had shown by his words and actions how little he valued her, who'd worked such a fundamental alteration in her with the uncomplicated power of his masculine sexuality.

Dragging her eyes and her mind away from him, she looked about with not entirely simulated interest. In the four years she'd been away there had been considerable changes. Suburbia reached out even further along the motorway, inching ever closer to the Bombay Hills. She had forgotten how banana palms and hibiscuses in every backyard gave the huge sprawl a cheerful, subtropical air that alleviated the effect of wide areas of housing and the heavy traffic.

'Your parents live in Henderson, don't they?' Leo's voice broke into her thoughts.

'Yes.' Her mouth tightened. 'I was a westie girl.'

The pejorative term for a girl from the western areas of Auckland, commonly held to be an amorphous mass of soulless housing with no centre and no culture beyond the car, came cynically from her lips.

Leo shrugged. 'It has a lot to offer. The Waitakere hills are the nearest forest area of Auckland, the vineyards and wineries have their own special appeal, and the west coast has some of the most magnificent black-sand beaches in the world.'

'I wouldn't know,' she said drily. 'We didn't go to the beach much—my mother hated the way we tracked sand into the house—but when we did it was always to the eastern beaches, or the ones on the Manukau. She didn't like the west-coast beaches. Too dangerous.'

She expected him to be surprised, but of course he knew about her family. Without expression he said, 'You should have a look at them. They're wild and fierce and yes, people do drown off them every year, usually fools who take the Tasman Sea too lightly.' His voice revealed his contempt for fools. 'But they're gloriously untamed and exquisitely beautiful. You'd like them, I think.'

His words made Tansy uneasy. She didn't want to discover that he was capable of loving places. That subtly raw undernote in his voice made her wonder stupid things, like how he would say, 'You are beautiful', or 'I want you', or even 'I love you'.

And that was infinitely more dangerous than any west coast beach.

'I'm sure they are,' she said colourlessly.

She knew the Dacres lived in Remuera, that suburb most favoured by the rich, so she expected him to turn off the motorway at Greenlane, but instead he drove on through Auckland and headed north.

Tansy felt a returning stir of fear. She demanded, 'Where are we going?'

'To our holiday home,' he said casually.

Of course he wouldn't take her to a house where she could just walk through the door and get a bus to the nearest police station. 'Where's that?'

'Just up the coast a little.' We waited until they were through Auckland and had reached the sea before saying, 'I don't think you will, but, just in case, don't try to convince Grace that I've kidnapped you.'

Strangely enough, such an action hadn't occurred to her. Tansy didn't really think that she could harass a sick woman, but she said smartly, 'What makes you think I won't try?'

'Intuition,' he said, and smiled mockingly at the disbelieving look she sent him. 'The dossier, Tansy. You spend some of your precious spare time singing at hospitals and old people's homes, and only a few days ago you risked losing your takings to help a man in the throes of a heart attack. I don't think you'll tell Grace.'

His detective had been very thorough. Fury surged through her in a white-hot tide. 'Did that bloody man stand by while someone robbed me?'

'He was the man who raced up and took over from you,' Leo said sharply. 'I didn't realise the money was stolen. How much did you lose?'

'Oh, it doesn't matter.' Tansy remembered the detective vividly, a burly, middle-aged man with quite a pleasant face. She'd been immensely relieved to see him because he knew what he was doing. It just went to show you couldn't trust anyone. She said acidly, 'Perhaps I'll make an exception to my general soft-heartedness for the Dacre family. You can't stop me from telling Grace anything I want to, and you know it.'

'I can.'

'How?'

'The usual way,' he said indifferently. 'By threats.'

She flashed him a slow, malicious smile. 'There's no way you can threaten me.'

He drove into a pull-off overlooking a river that wound green as bottle-glass between steep hills to a bay where the huge rounded domes of pohutukawa trees glowed like vast crimson jewels beneath the fierce sun, contrasting vividly, unforgettably, with white sand and aquamarine sea. A sprinkle of small islands meandered up the coast towards Kawau, the biggest of them all; out

to sea with the tiny, misty dot of Cuvier Island, halfway
between the smooth bulk of Mount Moehau at the and
of the Coromandel peninsula and Great Barrier Island,
sixty miles away.

'It depends entirely on the threat. You fascinate me,'
he said thoughtfully. 'So small and yet so intense, so
vibrant. I want to find out what thoughts live behind
those tiger eyes, all the emotions so securely hidden
behind your pale, proud face.'

His voice flowed around her and through her, setting
free responses that made her feel jittery and exalted at
the same time.

'You don't want to want me, but it shows, Tansy.'

Mesmerised, her heart thumping in her breast, she
tasted a poisonous cocktail of desire mixed with humiliation. She drew a jagged breath and covered her eyes
with her hands.

'It's quite normal and natural,' he said quietly. 'You've
done your best to hide it from everyone including
yourself, but you have desires and feelings and needs.
Why don't you let them free rein?'

She knew what the threat was. Diabolical, her
wounded heart cried noiselessly. If she told Grace he'd
kidnapped her, he'd use this obsession she was devel-
oping, seduce her into an affair—and in a moment of
blinding and horrifying revelation she knew that she
would not be able to resist.

Last night she had tasted a tiny draught of passion;
now he was offering the whole deadly cup. If he used
her own sexuality and her weakness against her, she
would be left with a shattered self-image and a broken
heart.

Because she could not surrender to lust and then walk
away. Tansy did not do things by halves. She had given
herself to her music with all the passion she had in her
because it was safer than falling in love. Some primal

instinct had warned her that she wouldn't be able to hold back or temper her emotions with practicality and common sense as others could.

And although she had told herself that she despised him, some secret, camouflaged part of her heart had been slowly falling a little bit in love with him. This threat, conveyed with all the lethal delicacy of a rapier, told her yet again that he wasn't worth it.

'I never had any intention of telling her,' she said curtly, her self-derision so intense that she didn't care if he saw it.

He didn't accept his victory with grace. 'Or of telling her that Ricky is on drugs?'

'No.'

He nodded, a lean hand twisting the starter key. 'Grace thinks he's going through an adolescent bad patch.' The big car purred out on to the road.

'You mean you convinced her,' she said remotely.

He shrugged. 'I'll do anything I have to. If she knew he was on drugs I think she'd give up and die.'

Only now did Tansy understand just how much he would do for his stepmother's peace of mind. He would even seduce a woman he didn't like, a woman he thought had been a streetwalker.

Before long they turned off the main highway, winding eastwards down a narrow metal road which dwindled into a drive. Eventually it debouched on to a beach sheltered from the easterlies by a couple of islands. A farmhouse half a mile away at the far end of the beach was not going to be a source of help. Tansy frowned at the wooden jetty extending across the white sand to the gentle waters of the bay. At the end, steps ran down to a tethered boat. Two large blackbacked gulls waddled away from the car along the weathered planks. As Leo got out, one yarped at them and took off, instantly transformed to a creature of power and grace in the air.

'Come on,' Leo said, unlocking the door. 'Don't bother to run away; the Schedewys are out for the day.'

Tansy said between her teeth, 'Watch your back, because one day I'm going to see you suffer for this.'

'I believe you,' he said. 'The Spanish have a proverb—"Take what you want, says God, then pay for it". I'm ready to pay.'

A cryptic note in his voice made her look sharply up into the arrogant, handsome face. He was a master at keeping it free from any betraying expression, but she suspected he might be a little less confident than normal.

The boat was a cross between a launch and a small barge. 'Which island are we going to?' she asked as he carried two suitcases down the wharf, leaving her with her guitar.

'The nearest.'

No hope of swimming to shore. It had to be at least a mile from land.

He kept her close by him while he switched on the engine; he knew exactly how to get the boat off the wharf, moving with the confident ease of experience. Tansy sat quietly as the vessel chugged in a pedestrian fashion out of the bay. In spite of the angry turmoil of outrage and frustration roiling inside her, a gleam of pleasure lifted her spirits. There was something about islands, something otherworldly, a feeling that the normal rules and strictures no longer applied.

Anything could happen on an island.

And in spite of her unqualified refusal to like anything he liked, this island was everything one should be. As it grew larger and larger she feasted her eyes on it, from the rocky eminence of its highest point to the slice of beach backed by the house. Pohutukawas fringed the shores and climbed the little hill, their crimson and scarlet flowers rich and radiant in the hot northern sun. Behind them a remnant of the native forest was canopied by taraires with an underbrush of shrubs and shorter trees emphatically set off by nikau palms and the feathery grace of ponga treeferns. It had a serene, primeval beauty that tugged at Tansy's heart.

Too small to farm, the island had been left in its natural state except for one bay, where she could pick out a green lawn behind the sprawl of pohutukawa trees that protected the house from sea winds. Not that many would get there; the island's position in the straggling archipelago that wandered up the coast ensured that any winds would be tempered by the influence of the land.

She had seen these islands from the mainland, but it had never occurred to her that people actually owned them. Like the well-cut clothes he wore, like the school he'd attended and his air of complete self-assurance, the island emphasised how very different Leo Dacre was from the rest of New Zealand.

Sheer, rapturous pleasure caught at Tansy's heart. She loved the sound of cicadas that zithered across the bay when the engine was cut and the boat nosed smoothly into the jetty beneath a rocky headland, the tang of salt in the lazy air, the glimpses of water between the twisted and gnarled trunks and branches of the pohutukawas. A northern summer, warm and potent and fiercely evocative; she had forgotten so much, and she had forgotten nothing.

'It looks very still,' Leo said as he came up on deck. 'Usually someone comes down to meet us.'

But no one came, and there was no call of welcome from the house.

Frowning, he said curtly, 'Come on,' and set off along the hard wooden planks of the jetty.

Guitar in hand, Tansy followed him. He waited for her where the jetty ended at a narrow roadway curving beneath the low cliff towards the house.

'You're someone who was kind to Ricky in Wellington and who now needs some peace and quiet,' he said calmly, holding out his hand for the case.

She lifted her brows. 'Won't your stepmother smell a rat when you mention Rick?'

'Why should she? She's never been a suspicious woman. I rang her the night before last to tell her that I had found you, and was bringing you home. She was thrilled. Of course, she'll want to know all about him. You can earn your keep by telling her.'

Rigidly, because she could control her fury no other way, she said, 'Is your stepmother accustomed to you bringing home stray women?'

'Not as a normal thing, no, but she won't object.'

'Because I took Rick in? Or because you are the great Leo Dacre?'

He gave her a sideways look. 'Even if you hadn't met him she'd be happy enough to entertain a guest of mine because she loves me,' he said simply.

What would it be like to have someone love you like that? In her most lacklustre voice, Tansy said, 'Some people have all the luck.' She walked around him and set off across newly mown lawns towards the house.

It was long and low and far from new, but it was well maintained, and the gardens looked as though they had a caretaker in residence. Tansy pretended to gaze around but saw very little beyond the fact that it was beautiful.

Grace Dacre didn't look ill. A tall, elegant woman with fine-drawn, aristocratic features and Rick's eyes, she was a little pale, but that could have been because she had been sleeping when they arrived. She certainly didn't seem to be expecting bad news.

Leo introduced Tansy, and to her intense embarrassment Grace seized the hand she extended and wept, 'So you did bring her back! Oh, Leo, thank you so much, darling!'

Just as though she had been a parcel, Tansy thought, but her heart melted at the older woman's distress, and instead of following her instinctive desire to pull away, she let her hand lie resistless in the chilly, beringed fingers.

'Oh, how was Ricky when you saw him last?' his mother asked urgently. 'Where did you meet him? Leo says you don't know where he is now, but I hoped—— We've been frantic, not knowing where he was or how he was living. One hears such awful things...'

Her voice trailed off. Tansy said robustly, 'He was fine. He found a job two days a week as a gardener.'

'A *gardener*?'

'He didn't know anything about it but he was willing to try, and the chap wanted muscles rather than skill. He didn't have them at first, but he soon developed them.' Rick had been rather proud of himself for getting that job.

His mother managed to conceal her astonishment, but she was beginning to see the implications of the situation. Hastily hidden speculation replaced that first pleading demand in her expression. 'He—stayed with you?' she asked tentatively.

'Yes. He was my boarder.' Tansy hoped her voice was firm enough to convince Rick's mother that she was no seducer of teenage boys.

The older woman's eyes sought Leo's. They exchanged a look that made Tansy prickle with resentment, before Mrs Dacre said, 'And what do you do, Tansy?'

When exactly the same note threaded Paula Farquharson's voice at the nightclub, Tansy had bristled. It was not condescension, exactly, more an assurance so deep that the owners didn't know they had it. In some subtle fashion it divided the world into two groups: the Dacres and their friends and family—and the rest.

But Grace Dacre was sick, and she was trying very hard to disguise her fear. For the first time Tansy understood how truly afraid the woman was for her son.

Because she had survived running away herself, and because she knew that Rick was all right, she'd been able to downplay his mother's terror. Leo, too, had a pretty good idea that Rick was in no immediate danger. But Grace thought him debauched, or dead.

Retrieving her hand, Tansy told her calmly, 'I've just finished a bachelor's degree in musical composition at Victoria University. Next year I'm going to begin my master's.'

'Oh,' the woman said blankly.

'And to earn money I busk,' Tansy finished.

Mrs Dacre was completely taken aback. 'I see. Is that where you met Ricky?'

The vulnerability that flashed nakedly in her eyes undermined Tansy's defensiveness even further. Grace Dacre might have pampered her son to the point of foolishness, but now Tansy knew why, and had seen the ravages fear and insecurity had wrought, she couldn't ignore the woman's obvious pain.

'Yes,' she said gently. 'I was singing at the railway station when I saw him. He'd just got off the train and didn't know where to go, so I offered him a bed for the night. We got on well, so he stayed.'

'Thank you. And you must think I'm terrible, catechising you like this, but we haven't known where Ricky was—he ran away from school, you know.' Her mouth quivered.

'Yes, I know,' Tansy said quietly, refusing to look at Leo. 'The day before he got to Wellington.'

Grace groped for the back of a chair. Unselfconsciously, Leo supported her until the incipent tears dried up and she was able to speak again.

She gave him a grateful, affectionate smile and said thickly, 'I wish he had thought he could come home. But as he didn't, I'm glad he found someone to—to offer him a base. And thank you for coming to see me, Tansy. How long did you say he stayed with you?'

'A couple of months.'

The older woman said, 'And you don't know where he is now?'

Tansy flashed a swift, sharp glance at Leo. He met it with an inexorable, level stare. Just once, she thought bitterly, she'd see him stripped of that ironclad self-possession. Just once, and she'd be happy.

'No,' she said, trying to soften the word and failing completely.

It was acutely distressing to see the sudden hope extinguished, the valiant attempt to smile. Guilt washed over Tansy.

In spite of her attempts to control her expression, Grace's face crumpled. 'Well, I'm sure he'll contact us soon,' she said, steadying her voice with an obvious effort. 'So you're going to stay with us for a while. I'm afraid it won't be a very social time——'

'Tansy isn't a very social person,' Leo interposed. 'She just wants to lie on the beach and compose her latest symphony. Don't you, Tansy?' Ostensibly it was a question; however, the note of warning in the words transformed them into a threat.

'It sounds wonderful,' she said stiffly.

'I've never met a person who writes music,' Mrs Dacre said, as though she were a strange, newly discovered form of wild animal. 'You must tell me all about it.'

She was a nice woman, but Tansy could see why Rick had grown up expecting the world to cater to his demands.

And if their mutual father had been anything like Leo, Tansy thought with a grimness that startled her, she understood where Rick had inherited the fortitude to overcome his addiction.

Grace Dacre put on a brave face, but there was a stillness about her, a momentary hesitation as though she expected pain each time she moved, that made Tansy uneasy.

'I think you should rest now,' Leo said firmly. 'Tansy and I want to swim, so we'll leave you in peace and quiet. Shall I get Frankie?'

Frankie Livingston turned out to be a distant cousin, a tall, gaunt woman who lived with Grace, and while they were on the island acted as housekeeper and cook. After being introduced to her Tansy decided that she was a much tougher nut than her employer. Certainly she looked from Leo's impassive face to Tansy's with something like anger, and her greeting was distinctly cool.

Not that Tansy cared. She wasn't here because she wanted to be, so they could think what they liked. Already Mrs Dacre was wondering whether Tansy was a scarlet woman who had seduced her son.

Frankie swept Mrs Dacre off, saying over her shoulder, 'Leo, do you mind showing Miss Ormerod to her room?'

'Of course not. Come on, Tansy, it's along here.'

Once out of earshot, Tansy said frigidly, 'I'd just as soon you didn't make arrangements for me, thank you.'

'Would you? I must remember that, if ever I want to please you.'

She cast him a black look and saw to her extreme irritation that he was smiling again. But then, why wouldn't Leo Dacre smile?

'I don't want to swim,' she said, fighting a deep desolation that appeared out of nowhere.

'Then lie in the shade of a pohutukawa tree.'

'I don't want to do that, either.' She faced him, her eyes cold and accusing. 'I've got no clothes except the ones I had on yesterday, and you expect me to stay here as your prisoner until you decide I can go home. Damn you, I should be working. I need that money for next year.'

'I told you I'd make it financially worth your while. As for clothes, I'm not totally insensitive. There are some in the wardrobe of your room.'

'I don't want you to pay me,' she snapped. 'I pay my own way. And I wouldn't wear clothes you bought me——'

His eyes narrowed. 'Keep your voice down,' he ordered succinctly, 'and save your prudish little principles for yourself. Grace is going to wonder if she sees you in those clothes all the time.'

She looked down at the jeans and the terracotta T-shirt and realised that of course they weren't her own clothes, either. 'What did you do with mine?' she asked belligerently.

'Threw them away,' he said. 'They were only fit for the dump.'

Sparks shot through her bloodstream and for a wild second she could have flung herself at him and punched him where it hurt most, slapped his handsome face, bitten him hard until she drew blood. The naked violence of her emotions terrified her.

'Why do you wear clothes like that? They make you look like a crow,' he said cruelly.

'Because they were cheap,' she said between her teeth. 'Some people, Mr Rich Man, have to watch their money.'

He flung open a door and stood back, anger radiating from him like a cloud from a volcano, dark and forbidding and deadly dangerous.

Savagely satisfied, Tansy swept in front of him into the room.

It was small and sparse and pleasant, with a single bed along one wall and a white cane chair made comfortable by a chintz cushion striped in the same blue

and white of the spread. The dressing-table was cane,
too; Tansy didn't normally like cane furniture, but this
was old and looked just right. A shelf held a selection
of books ranging from children's classics to a couple of
the latest bestsellers. French windows opened out on to
a wide bricked terrace afroth with small flowering plants
where bees hummed. It stretched the full length of the
house, shaded in part by a brilliant scarlet bougainvillaea. Tansy stopped in the doorway and looked out,
and the hectic flush died from her skin.

Her eyes lingered on the velvety buds of the
pohutukawa trees across the lawn, appreciating the
moment a vagrant breeze ruffled the leathery leaves to
reveal the furred, silver undersides.

If only conditions were different, she would love
behind here.

'Thank you,' she muttered, staring straight ahead.

'Think nothing of it.' He spoke negligently, as though
she was nothing to him.

Tansy waited tensely until the door closed. Then, when
she was safe, she wriggled her shoulders, easing the strain
from her spine. A long, soundless sigh huffed from her
lips.

At first she refused to go across to the wardrobe, but
eventually vulgar curiosity got the better of her. Leo had
arranged for mostly holiday clothes in the earth tones
he obviously thought she should wear, olive and moss
and jade, bronze and coffee and peach, the turquoise
of the sea and the kingfisher-blue of the sky. There were
shirts and trousers and several dresses. Carefully arranged at the bottom were shoes, sneakers and casual
flats and sandals.

As though facing execution, she went across to the
tallboy and opened a drawer. Brand new underwear,
several pairs of shorts, and a couple of bathing suits
were neatly folded inside.

How had he organised it, and who had done the shopping? Was this why Frankie had looked at her with such chilly reserve? Tansy's finger traced the seam of a satin bra, flicked the tag back. Yes, the right size. How had he known that? The clothes she wore didn't reveal much of her body; that was one of the reasons she bought them. Such skill in judging a woman's intimate sizing indicated either a life spent in the trade, or experience. And as he certainly didn't own a lingerie shop, it had to be experience.

Something slow and feral and barbaric swept through her. Intellectually she'd accepted that there was very little Leo Dacre didn't know about women. This jealousy, this white-hot flood of fury was not even emotion: it was something physical, an outrage that was animal and instinctive.

How had he explained all these clothes?

Her smile was cynically mirthless. He probably hadn't. After all, if you were Leo Dacre, you didn't need to explain yourself.

From the corner of her eye she caught a movement; before she had time to think she turned to see what or who was walking across the lawn towards the beach. Leo, a towel over his shoulder, black bathing trunks clinging to lean hips, waved a careless hand as he swung beneath the pohutukawa branches and down the bank.

CHAPTER SIX

STRANGE and unusual sensations did strange and unusual things to Tansy's stomach and backbone. She felt a return of the reluctant, hidden heat in her cells, the sharp, ancient tug at the senses that was awareness.

No, it was more than awareness. It was desire.

She had felt it before, a sweet stirring in her blood, but this was different; this was fierce and primeval, an aching fever. She wanted Leo with an intensity that consumed self-control and left it bitter ashes in her mouth.

Her thin, strong hands, fingers callused from the guitar strings, clenched into fists as she turned away. She felt such an idiot. He had taken her for a fool, strung her along and then done this to her, yet she couldn't banish images of him from her brain. Wet from the shower, his sleek body had been poised with all the terrible beauty of a predator, his hard, angular face tough and keen as a warrior.

Relax, she told herself contemptuously. You're just the same as all the others, a sucker for a pretty face. Snatching a book that looked mildly interesting, she went out on to the terrace and collapsed into a recliner.

She was pretending to read when he came back. From the corners of her eyes she'd seen him walk up from the beach and across the lawn to his room, but kept her head adamantly lowered, hoping that he would take the hint. Of course, she should have known better.

'Your hair looks like a sunburst,' he remarked, lowering himself into a chair with the easy grace of a panther.

She lifted indifferent eyes. 'I'm reading,' she pointed out rudely.

'No, you're not. You're trying to read.'

Did he know how much he affected her? She surveyed him through her lashes, but although he looked amused there was no derision in his expression. Some rawness was soothed deep inside her. If he realised that far from being merely attracted to him she was rapidly becoming obsessed, her position here would become untenable.

Ostentatiously, she closed the book and put it in her lap, asking in her most neutral voice, 'Did you have something you wanted to discuss?'

'Yes, but not here, and not now. After dinner I'll suggest a walk along the beach, and you'll say yes.'

'What if I say no?'

'Don't,' he advised laconically.

Eyes glittering, Tansy got to her feet. Leo caught her hand as she stormed by, his tanned fingers forming a ring around the fragile bones of her wrist. They didn't hurt, but she couldn't go any further.

'I knew you were stubborn and arrogant,' he said, scanning her flushed face with half-closed eyes. 'It shows in your jaw and the impertinent little jut to your chin. I can understand that, because you've got something very few other people have. Just don't make the mistake of thinking that it's going to get you anywhere with me.'

To her profound astonishment he lifted her hand and turned it over and kissed the palm, his teeth grazing the soft skin there with passionate, sensuous skill.

Tansy's blood surged through her body. She had never thought of her hand as an erogenous zone, but his teeth summoned a clutch of liquid desire at the fork of her body, a subtle heaviness to her breasts, tightening the sensitive skin of her nipples into unbearable peaks.

Her hand jerked; she tugged, but he kept it against his mouth. Bemused by sensation, dazzled by her first real experience of desire, she felt her knees buckle and grabbed the back of his chair.

Time folded in on itself, brought the universe to a juncture where nothing else happened but the sun beating down on her head and his, kindling blue flames in the charcoal hair; she could see his lashes shading the high, autocratic sweep of his cheekbones, the straight blade of his nose, yet her whole attention was focused on his mouth against her hand, as though all other sense organs had shut down and she was able only to feel. Two fires, she thought dimly, the sun, and his touch.

'You have interesting hands,' he murmured, and the universe spun on its way.

White-hot wires pulled through her. This time she didn't try to free herself; she couldn't even lift her hand.

'You promised,' she croaked. Childish, but her brain had turned to sludge.

He held her hand in front of him, examining the long, slightly crooked fingers with their short nails. His lean forefinger touched the callus on her finger, rubbing it rhythmically. 'I like your hands,' he said, his voice deep and disciplined. 'They're strong and fine-boned and capable, just like you. And somehow that ferocious intensity that vibrates through you like the tides of life shows even in your hands.'

He looked up, catching her by surprise. Beneath his lashes his eyes shimmered green, polished and enigmatic. A little smile curled at his wide, cynical mouth as he let her go. Tansy immediately took a step backwards and pushed her hand behind her, hiding the palm with her fingers.

'Yes, I promised,' he said sardonically. 'So you're quite safe, at least until you leave here.'

He waited courteously, but when she couldn't think of anything sensible to say he went on, 'Amusing, isn't it, that of all the people in the world we two should want each other?'

She said in a gravelly voice, 'I hate it.'

His eyes held hers, brilliant, inscrutable, but the tiny flame that burned in their depths had the same origin as the one that seared through her. 'I know, but you don't need to worry. I keep my promises.' His smile hardened. 'Unless,' he added with a return to his usual drawl, 'you tell me you don't want me to.'

Slowly she shook her head, still holding her hand behind her like a toddler caught stealing from the biscuit tin.

'In that case,' he said smoothly, 'neither of us has anything to worry about, do we?'

With as much dignity as she could muster, Tansy walked into her room, staying there until dinner.

They ate at the table out on the terrace, but not even the magnificent view nor the quiet sounds of the waves nor the superb food could ease the strained atmosphere. Tansy knew she was the cause and the centre of the tension, and her anger with Leo for forcing her into this position increased.

Yet she too was strung up, although for different reasons. Busy trying to find some way of blocking that tense incident on the terrace from her consciousness, she was as quiet as Frankie Johnson, who ate with them, but said very little to the Dacres, and almost nothing to Tansy.

Mrs Dacre, however, spoke enough for both of them. She wanted to hear, in all-encompassing detail, what Rick had said, where he had gone, how he had behaved, in the time he spent with Tansy. She wanted to know how he felt and what he looked like, her questions dancing around in a way that made Tansy distinctly uneasy. Did she suspect Ricky, as they all called him, of taking drugs?

No, Tansy decided before the end of the meal. Although Rick's mother was worried sick about him, it wasn't drugs she suspected. She had almost convinced herself that it was merely a particularly tumultuous stage he was going through. Leo had done a good PR job there. Mrs Dacre even seemed to believe that her son's behaviour was understandable, almost inevitable, because, as she confided, 'Ricky is very sensitive, you know.'

Although he'd appeared as sensitive as most seventeen-year-old boys, a breed more noted for roughhousing and horse-play than delicacy of emotion, Tansy nodded.

Grace Dacre's need was understandable, but Tansy found the inquisition stressful, especially as it soon became obvious that she wanted to know exactly what relationship she and Rick had. Tansy answered honestly, emphasising the total lack of any sexuality.

Whether she managed to reassure her or not, Tansy couldn't see. She was acutely conscious of Leo on the other side of the table, saying very little yet somehow managing by his interpolations to direct the conversation.

Choosing every word while trying to appear open and candid so that the older woman didn't guess she was hiding things wore Tansy out. By the time dinner was over she felt like a limp cloth. Another thing, she decided malevolently, to chalk up against Leo.

Bringing her here had been a clever move. She had only needed fortitude to refuse him, but watching Mrs Dacre turn her head so that no one would see the tears in eyes the exact blue of Rick's, hearing the quaver in her voice when she spoke of her son, aching at her determination not to admit that something could be seriously wrong, was a torture more exquisite than anything else Leo could have devised.

After dinner he said casually, 'Come for a walk, Tansy.'

She hesitated, her eyes smoky with secrets as she looked at him. His expression didn't alter.

Looking from one to the other, Mrs Dacre said diffidently, 'Yes, do go, Tansy. It's very pretty—we have some lovely sunsets.'

'Thank you,' Tansy said, and got to her feet.

He waited until they were walking side by side along the beach before saying, 'You did very well. I think you convinced Grace that Ricky is able to look after himself.'

'Why do you call him Ricky?'

'What's that got to do with anything? It's his name.'

'It's such a baby name, as though he's deliberately being kept in an inferior position.'

He swung up the bank and stood at the top, holding out a hand which she ignored. 'I suppose you think that sharing a bed with him makes you an expert on him?'

It took a moment for the coolly voiced observation to register fully. When it did, Tansy's nostrils flared and her eyes glowed golden. 'We did not sleep together,' she snapped.

'I've seen your room, remember? There's a double bed in it and nothing else.'

In a voice molten with rage she said, 'The chair unrolls into a mattress. Rick slept there. It was cramped and uncomfortable, but he didn't seem to mind, especially after he'd had a chance to see the way real street kids live.'

A track led up the rocky little hill behind the house. Blindly, still furious, she pushed past him and took off up it as though the devil was growling at her heels. At the top the hill fell steeply to low, red cliffs covered with scrub and small trees. Tansy arrived far too fast, and if Leo hadn't caught her from behind she could have taken a nasty tumble down the slope.

As it was she was dragged to a rapid halt by a punishing grip and held against a lean, taut body. 'Stupid little bitch!' Leo said furiously.

He turned her around and shook her, and then, so swiftly it took a second for her to resist, hauled her into his arms and kissed her.

It was hard and fierce and it went on for a long time. She yielded, her body surging with a lethal, heady combination of fury and desire.

'Bitch,' he said harshly, and kissed her again, and this time she couldn't stop herself from thrusting against him, seeking his strength and the heat of his body, her nostrils filled with his scent, her skin tingling, eagerly acceptant of the magic his mouth performed.

'Bastard,' she groaned, afire, when his mouth lifted.

He laughed, a hasty, broken sound, and bit the soft skin of her throat. It didn't hurt; he knew exactly what pressure to exert, she thought with a savage pang of anger for the other women whose willing submission had given him this experience.

'Don't,' she choked, but he laughed again, strong hands moving down her back to hold her hips remorselessly against him, so that the throbbing urgency of his need set off a thundering reaction through her.

She gasped, and once more her hips moved, sinuously, reflexively, striving for a surcease she had never known. She looked into a face made arrogant by a barbaric, raptor's exultation, the keen joy of conquest, a challenging desire that owed nothing to kindness or affection. He was beautiful in his power, awe-inspiring in the full glory of his masculinity.

An answering wildness soared to meet his; she shivered in its ferocity, buffeted by gales of emotion she didn't want, didn't understand, couldn't fight.

But she had to reject him, because there was no future for her in this. He was using her. Soon he would ask again where Rick was, and, forgetting honour, she might tell him.

She willed herself to be still, to freeze the violence, to let it wash through her in its tide of fire and light and sensation, and then ebb, down and down and down, until at last it was nothing more than embers.

'How do you do that?' he asked caustically, letting her go as though the touch of her soiled his hands. 'Just kill passion like that? It's a trick worth having.'

'It's a trick I've had to learn,' she said with a bitter little smile. Growing up in a family where her one talent was actively decried, she had soon realised that it was unwise to reveal her emotions.

How long ago had she discovered that excitement was to be controlled? When she first ran to her mother with a tune she had made up, and found that Pam didn't want to hear it? Perhaps it had started then. She had worshipped Miss Harding because she too had shared this hunger for music, the exaltation it could bring, but to Miss Harding it was only the music that mattered, nothing else. Tansy had soon realised that her mentor didn't care about the child, only for the talent.

So Tansy had trained herself to watch and observe, to hold back, to keep a lid on her emotions. Just as well, too, for without that inner control she might have given in to the untamed sweetness of her responses.

'Stupid of me,' Leo said, stepping back, his eyes hooded as he looked at her white face. 'I suppose you had to learn to cut off.'

For a moment she didn't understand what he meant. Then she understood; he was referring to the year she had spent supposedly on the street.

'Why are you so interested?' she asked coarsely. 'Does the thought turn you on?'

His eyes narrowed. 'No,' he said softly. 'I'm not in the least turned on by the thought of a sixteen-year-old girl forced into prostitution. Sickened would probably be a better way of describing my feelings. I have normal sexual instincts, not perverted ones.'

No doubt he was revolted because for a few seconds he wanted a woman he thought to be a reformed prostitute. Good; it made things a lot safer for her.

'Have you had counselling?' he asked.

She lifted her lashes and gave him a long, sarcastic look. 'How would I pay for counselling? Do you think I need rescuing just because I say no? You've got a high view of your attractions.'

To her amazement dark colour licked along his cheekbones. He said tightly, 'You were responding, I know you were, and then you pulled away and cut off.'

'A kiss is one thing,' she said casually and cruelly. 'Groping is another.'

'Groping?' He astonished her again by bursting into laughter, his handsome head thrown back as he gave way to real amusement, real mirth.

Tansy eyed him carefully, hiding her bewilderment with what she hoped was a suitably hard-boiled expression. She didn't know much about men, but she was pretty sure that few would have thought her remark funny.

When he'd stopped he said comfortably, 'You sound like a schoolmistress, such a prim little face and such prim words. I wonder about you, Tansy.'

She didn't want him wondering about her. He was too quick, too clever, too able to draw inferences and fathom things out. Shrugging, she said calmly, 'Enjoy slumming, do you? Why are we here? What did you want to tell me that you couldn't say back at the house?'

He looked at her consideringly, some trace of that amusement barely softening his mouth. 'I enjoy being with you,' he said.

Angry colour scorched her cheeks. He was mocking her and she couldn't find any reply scathing enough. Eventually she said, 'I'm going back now.'

'All right.' He spoke as though conferring permission, his offhand tone of voice grating unbearably on her nerves.

'Before I do,' she said, knowing it wouldn't work, 'why don't you give up? You must have realised that I'm not going to tell your stepmother anything, so why not let me go? If you do, I won't tell the police. I'll just go back to Wellington and we'll forget we ever met, that you ever kidnapped me.'

'Nice try,' he said admiringly. 'Unfortunately, I don't trust you an inch. You stay here. You're the only clue we have to Ricky's whereabouts.'

Woodenly, she skirted around him and went off back down the track, holding on to her self-control by the thinnest of margins. That kiss had turned her brain to slush, left her shaky and weak, and despising herself. It wasn't ever going to happen again.

There was no respite when she got back, either. Grace Dacre was lying in wait for her in the sitting-room like a pale but determined spider, desperation in her eyes.

It was sheer torture to have to dredge up incidents to convince her that Rick had been all right. Tansy wearied of picking her words carefully, because of course there had been times when Rick had not been all right, when his need for the drug he was addicted to had sent him over the border into irrationality.

Eventually, when she had completely run out of anecdotes, she yawned and said, 'I'm sorry, I'm afraid I'm quite tired.'

'No, *I'm* sorry. I've been very selfish and you're a darling to have put up with it,' Mrs Dacre said, remorse shadowing her beautiful eyes so that Tansy saw why Leo and Rick loved her. She sighed. 'If only I knew he was all right. If he feels he needs the time away I wouldn't want him to come back, but it's the uncertainty, the not knowing, that's so hard. Now, don't you go worrying about me—you're been dragged into our affairs enough. I don't think I've told you how very grateful I am for putting your own plans on hold and coming all the way up here to reassure me. Off you go to bed, Tansy. Breakfast is around eight, but if you're like Leo and wake up starving at six do help yourself from the kitchen.'

Feeling lower than a louse, Tansy went along to her room where she undressed and pulled on a blue seer-sucker dressing-gown. The bathroom was just along the passage; it had been prettily and recently renovated. Even if she hadn't known who lived here, she thought as she washed and cleaned her teeth, she'd guess it was someone who had a lot of money, although the rooms weren't sleek and glossy and obviously expensive. This house had a mellow, settled look, its decorating done by someone with the casual skill of excellent taste.

After washing out the underclothes she had worn she carried them back to her room. She was not going to wear more clothes than she needed to; she couldn't do much to defy Leo, but she would make what protest she could.

She took off the dressing-gown and hung it up, then switched off the light and sat down on the bed, her hands clasped between her knees as she unflinchingly recalled those moments in Leo's arms when fury and disillusion had fuelled her hunger, transforming desire into a stu-pefying, reckless passion.

She wanted to make him suffer, she thought with sudden bleak insight. She wanted him to want her with such intensity that he thought nothing of her back-ground, nothing of her presumed past, because they were irrelevant to him.

Why? Because he had slipped through the barriers she had set up against the claims of the world and made off with her most closely guarded treasure, her independence.

Her hands writhed together, were reduced to stillness by force of will. Was this unwilling, mindless need love?

How did she know? What was love? The O'Briens had seemed quite fond of each other, but she had left before she could understand them with an adult insight. Certainly she had never noticed any sign of the sort of desperation that gripped her now. They had seemed easy with each other, her father perhaps a little in awe of her mother.

Her knowledge of love was purely theoretical. Oh, she had seen affairs burgeon and flourish at university, but she had never understood how a perfectly sensible woman could suddenly start blushing and simpering when confronted by a perfectly ordinary man.

So she was not ready to deal with this aberration. She simply didn't know what such fiery violence meant. It didn't seem like love to her; if it resembled anything, it was a bonfire, flaming fiercely and then dying as quickly, all the heat and light and excitement quenched by bitter cold and darkness.

While she had been thinking music had been hovering at the edge of her consciousness, dancing, forming patterns in her brain. She pulled the pad Leo had given her the night before from the drawer, switched on the bedside lamp and began to set notes down, playing tentatively with motifs and phrases until the ideas came to fruition. Curled up against the pillow, she wrote rapidly, without erasures, the music pouring from her, finding its way through the frail barriers of her brain and fingers on to the paper.

She had no idea how long she wrote, or even what she had written; it seemed as though something had captured her brain and taken over her responses, but eventually she put down the pen and sat quietly, staring with a startled lassitude at the darkness that had filled the garden.

A knock on the door made her look around slowly. 'Yes?' she said huskily.

Instead of an answer it opened to reveal Leo with a tray in his hands. He walked straight through and out on to the terrace, saying casually, as though the uninhibited sensuality of the evening's encounter had never happened, 'Tea. You look as though you need it.'

Exhausted, Tansy followed him without protest. She collapsed into a chair and said lethargically, 'I've been writing.'

'I know. I saw your light and came along half an hour ago. Since then I've been sitting out here waiting for you to finish.'

A resurgence of the vulnerability she had felt when she realised he'd watched her sleeping made her flush. 'I hate being spied on,' she said, but without any real heat.

'I didn't watch you,' he said lazily, pouring her tea. 'I just waited.'

'Why?'

There was no light, merely the glow from the lamp in her room, so she couldn't catch the expression on his dark face too clearly, but she thought he looked a little taken aback.

'I wasn't ready for bed,' he said, 'and we need to talk. Drink up.'

The tea was wonderful, hot and fresh-tasting, just the way she liked it. Tansy said, 'Aren't you having any?'

He showed her a glass, almost empty. 'I'll finish this,' he said.

Warmth, unexpected and sweet, flooded through her. She drank some more of the tea before saying shyly, 'It was a nice thought.'

In the darkness his soft laughter stroked along her nerves. 'I do have nice thoughts now and then. And I was intrigued.'

'Intrigued?'

'Yes. Like most people I'm enormously fascinated by those who can create beauty.'

Colour heated her skin at the unexpected compliment. She said quietly, 'I think almost everyone starts with that ability. Sometimes I wonder whether we kill it in our children. I know——' She stopped, wondering how she had let one kind gesture loosen her tongue to this extent.

'Didn't your foster-parents understand?'

'No,' she said, her voice muted. She looked across the space that separated them. Perhaps it was the pernicious effect of islands, but she found herself wanting to tell him more than she had ever told anyone else.

'Were they unkind?'

She laughed ironically. 'No. I think I could have coped with unkindness. They tried—oh, how they tried to like me. I was four when I first went there, and I knew even then they were trying. They'd adopted Michelle and Jason when they were babies, and they fitted in perfectly. I don't really know why they took me in; perhaps because they thought the five years between the other two was too big a gap. Anyway, it didn't work out. I didn't look like them, I didn't think like them, and we certainly didn't have anything in common. They thought I was weird, and before too long I began to believe it too.'

He· said something under his breath, adding aloud, 'It's a wonder you didn't end up with a massive complex.'

'Miss Harding saved me. She was convinced I had talent, and she was hell-bent on doing something about it. She encouraged me.'

'Did your foster-parents mind?'

Trust him to pick up on the nuances. She said sadly, 'Yes. They'd done their best for me, saved me from a life in institutions, and I was ungrateful enough not to love them for it. Michelle was pretty and cheeky and loving, and Jason settled in as though he had been born to them, but I was not an affectionate, cuddly child. My mother didn't like Miss Harding—she thought she gave me ideas above my station.'

'I suppose she was jealous,' he said. 'You and your Miss Harding shared something she couldn't.'

'Perhaps,' she said non-committally. 'I know I was the despair of her life. I didn't want to play with dolls, I wasn't interested in clothes or boys or dancing or gossip, all the things she liked talking about. I was rude and abrupt and ungracious, and I had this disconcerting way of going off into daydreams. I was hopeless at school, too.'

'Were you? You don't strike me as unintelligent.'

She shrugged. The tea was relaxing her, yet it had a mildly stimulating effect, too. At that moment she could think of nowhere better to be than sitting on this terrace, the sound and scent of the sea about her, talking to Leo.

'Fundamentally, I was bored. I used to read most of the time. I lived for my music lessons.' She had told him enough; too much, probably. 'What about you?' she asked. 'What were you like as a child?'

She saw a swift white flash which was a smile. 'Turn about?' he mocked. 'Depressingly ordinary, I'm afraid.'

Tansy didn't believe that for a moment. 'Where did you grow up?' she asked.

'In Auckland. I had a very happy childhood, although my mother was never strong after I was born. She died when I was seven.'

'That's tough.'

'Yes, I thought the bottom had fallen out of my world. I know it's trite, but that honestly was how it felt, as though some wicked being had torn away half my life. Still, I had my father, and we were good mates. He wasn't particularly demonstrative, but he loved me. After a few years he married Grace, and although I was suspicious at first I soon realised that she was just the sort of stepmother a boy should have. She never tried to be a mother; well, she wasn't old enough to be a mother to me. It was like having a big sister, one who laughed and played with me and loved me.'

Which explained the different quality to their relationship. Tansy felt another pang of guilt, realising how ill Grace was; she looked much older than she must be.

'So life went on just the same,' Leo said, 'except that we lived in Christchurch and soon there was Ricky.'

Tansy braced herself, but he went on without pause, 'He was such a bright little kid, happy and eager and affectionate, even when he was damned near at death's door. I was too grown up, I felt, to be interested in babies, but the first time he came home from the hospital Grace gave him to me to carry into the house, and one of his hands clasped my finger, and I swear he smiled at me. I had no defences after that.'

Tansy swallowed. She was getting dragged deeper and deeper into the mire, and feeling worse and worse about it.

'Finished your tea?' Leo asked.

Tansy nodded. 'Yes. Thank you,' she said colourlessly. 'It was a super idea.'

'Good.' He got up and collected the things together on the tray. 'You look very fetching in that nightgown,' he said matter-of-factly.

It was some indication of her bemused state that Tansy had completely forgotten she had on only a nightgown, even though it was a pretty cotton one that covered more than a sunfrock would.

'Goodnight,' he said, laughter and something else in his voice as he left the terrace.

She fled into her room and turned off the light. Oh, Rick, she thought as she slid between the sheets, you didn't know what you were doing when you made me promise not to tell!

But of course he had known; that was why he'd extracted the promise from her. He knew his brother only too well.

Strangely enough, the following few days were peaceful. After Wellington's weather it was delicious to bask in the hot northern sun, although, she was amused to see on television one night, the weather had improved immensely in Wellington once she left it! Tansy let the tranquillity soak into her soul, allowing herself to drift with lazy inertia, not looking to the future, not thinking of the past.

The only rock in the smooth current of her days was Grace, who seemed to get thinner and more febrile every day, and Frankie, whose attitude of aloof disdain didn't alter. Although Tansy told herself she didn't care, it hurt.

The temptation to reveal Rick's whereabouts became unbearable. She was devoutly thankful she had rung the camp; it was only the leader's frank evaluation of Rick's progress that kept her mute.

Still convinced that her silence was best for Rick, she now understood that no decision stood on its own. It had been easy when she didn't know Grace; now, having

seen her ill and imprisoned by her nervy, slightly neurotic fears, terrified about her son's welfare, Tansy could
no longer comfort herself with a clear-cut and rather
smug verdict.

She was constantly in Grace's company, because Leo
wasn't around much. He spent most of his time in the
office.

There were no more impassioned kisses. He made her
swim with him, insisted that she join them after dinner
on the terrace, talked with her and gave her books he
thought she might like to read, even ordered a stack of
CDs for her in case she was suffering from a lack of
music, and introduced her to the caretakers and their
family of two high-school sons, but he never said anything personal to her.

Tansy was, she told herself sturdily, relieved at his distance. She was also, she admitted when her defences were
down, piqued. It seemed she wasn't the only one who
could turn off so completely.

Then one afternoon a yacht glided smoothly into the
bay and nudged against the wharf.

'Oh, it's the Sullivans,' Grace said, brightening.
'They're old friends.'

They were very pleasant, very affable. They kissed
Grace and Leo, nodded at Frankie, and shook hands
with Tansy with swiftly veiled curiosity. After staying
around for the minimum time, Tansy ignored Leo's level,
forbidding gaze to excuse herself as Frankie had done.

She went into the kitchen and in spite of Frankie's
covert discouragement helped her prepare lunch before
going to her room. As she passed the wide double doors
out on to the terrace she heard Jessica Sullivan ask carefully, 'Just who is this Tansy? Anyone we know?'

Grace said swiftly, 'No, just a nice girl, a friend
of Ricky's.'

Tansy stole quietly down the hall, but not fast enough to keep out the young woman's high-pitched laugh. 'Oh. He's starting young, just like Leo!'

'No, no, it's nothing like that.' Grace sounded flustered. 'She's up here for a holiday.'

'Is Ricky here, then?'

Damn the woman, why didn't she shut up?

'No,' Grace said firmly, 'he's in the South Island.'

Did she *know*? Tansy took another step. The Sullivan woman said, 'But he'll be here for Christmas, surely?'

'Probably not,' Grace said on a sigh.

Jessica said earnestly, 'Oh, you will miss him, but the young have to stretch their wings. Rather rough of him to dump a stranger on you, though. At Christmas time, too, but boys don't think, the wretches. How long is she here for?'

'I'm not sure,' Grace said, a note of distress in her voice.

The younger woman continued, 'You'd have thought she'd understand that nobody wants total strangers in their house over Christmas. Especially when you're not too well. Some people just don't know how to behave, do they?'

Tansy's hackles rose. She half turned, then swung back as Grace said firmly, 'She's a very nice girl.'

Oddly touched, Tansy went along to her room and sat down, looking at her trembling hands. There had been real concern in the younger woman's voice, and anger. The awful thing about it was that Tansy agreed with Jessica Sullivan. Grace didn't need her there; they had too little in common for her to be anything but a nuisance. Grace only put up with her because she was her sole link to Rick.

The yacht stayed for three days, days in which Tansy learned that Jessica Sullivan knew everyone of any importance in New Zealand, and that, like Leo, she and her rather characterless husband were related to most of them.

Tansy acquitted the woman of trying to make her uncomfortable; she made pleasant conversation whenever Tansy was around, but Tansy found it almost impossible to talk to her. She resented being made to feel a cuckoo in the nest, yet the fury she felt with Leo for putting her in such a position no longer had quite such a natural outlet. She understood his reasons, although she couldn't forgive him for it.

She took a sour pleasure in alternating her two outfits. Jessica Sullivan looked at her with incredulity and Grace with a kind of pitying sympathy she found utterly galling, but, infuriatingly, Leo didn't seem to notice.

Watching Grace deteriorate day by day was slow torture. Tansy found herself avoiding everyone, keeping to her room, going for walks alone.

She was enormously relieved when the Sullivans finally sailed away. After watching the topmost part of the sail disappear behind the little headland, she turned to go into her room, when a buzzing in the sky caught her attention. Within a minute the small amphibian aircraft that served the islands of the gulf came noisily into the bay, planing along the surface of the water like a great, stubby water beetle.

'Who now?' she muttered crossly.

Nobody arrived, however. Instead, Grace and Leo left on it and spent the whole long, hot day away, only returning when the sun began its western descent behind the hills of the mainland. Grace went straight to bed, cared for by a silent Frankie, and Leo locked himself into his office.

Tansy had watched them fearfully as they were rowed ashore from the amphibian, but neither Grace's face nor Leo's told her anything. Now she couldn't sleep. She was sitting uncomfortably on the terrace, very aware of the light from the office, when Frankie came out and walked heavily across to the edge of the terrace, staring out at the swooping branches of the pohutukawa trees.

'Is she all right?' Tansy asked from the depths of the recliner.

Frankie whirled around. 'No, she's not,' she said. She had been crying; the sob was still in her voice. Perhaps it was grief that made her continue angrily, 'She has to have another operation, and even then the surgeon's only hopeful, he can't promise anything.'

'I'm sorry.' Tansy felt sick.

The older woman made a disbelieving noise. 'Then why don't you go?' she asked bitterly. 'Can't you see you're not wanted here?'

The temptation to tell her why she didn't go was strong enough to open Tansy's mouth, but she closed it with a snap. This had nothing to do with Frankie.

So she said quietly, 'I'm here because Leo wants me here. No,' as Frankie began to speak, 'I don't think you should say anything you might regret when you're feeling better.'

She got to her feet and walked into her bedroom, to sit on the side of the bed and wonder whether she should ring the camp.

If she did, it would blow Rick's cover once and for all, whether he was ready to leave or not. Leo would know the moment the bill came whom she had been ringing, and once that happened, Rick would be out of there in no time flat.

She had never felt so alone before, never been so worried about the results of her actions. Whatever she did, she would be harming someone.

Why hadn't Leo told Grace that Tansy knew where Rick was? He was too astute not to see how much Grace's condition affected his reluctant prisoner; surely he knew that if he did tell the pressure would become intolerable?

Perhaps he had learned that Tansy could not be bullied into doing what she felt was wrong. It was Grace who would suffer most from Tansy's silence.

Primed by Rick's view of his mother, she hadn't expected to like Grace, but there was something essentially gallant about her that compelled respect. She had done her best to be a good hostess, striving to ensure that Tansy enjoyed herself. And although she might smother her son, Tansy could understand her behaviour now.

If Leo told her that Grace was dying, what would she do?

Eventually she went to bed, waking up the next morning with a decision made. She would insist on leaving. After breakfast she set her teeth and, ignoring the little voice that told her running away wasn't going to solve anything, tapped on the door of Leo's office.

He was opening letters. When she walked in he looked up, his eyes narrowing. 'What is it?'

Nervous tension made her brusque. 'I want to go.'

'No.' He spoke dispassionately, continuing to slit envelopes.

'Damn you, I hate it! Frankie still thinks I'm your mistress, and the Sullivans were totally condescending. I'm certainly not helping Grace.' With a strength she didn't know she possessed she reined back her anger. 'You must have realised by now that I'm not going to tell you anything, so why are you keeping me here?' she demanded.

'Because I wouldn't put it past you to disappear if I let you go.'

She stared at him with baffled fury. 'If I promised not to?'

He laughed, something ugly showing for a moment in the green depths of his eyes. 'Tell me why I should trust you.'

She had no answer to that.

He said, 'I'm not going to let you go, and I'm afraid there's nothing you can do or say to convince me otherwise.'

She said hotly, 'I haven't got any Christmas presents!'

He flung back his head and laughed. Losing her composure entirely, Tansy flew at him, strain stripping every shred of civilised behaviour from her. She had no idea what she was going to do, beyond wiping the laughter from his arrogant, laughing face.

He grabbed her wrists and shook her until she gasped, her eyes a pure, feline yellow beneath her lashes, spitting fire and fury.

'That's enough,' he said sharply. 'You can be as surly as you like, but you're not leaving the island until you tell me where Ricky is. Now get out.'

CHAPTER SEVEN

ANGER swamped by a great, black flood of self-pity, she slammed through the door and stormed down the hall towards the piano. Although old it was well-cared for, and she sat down to play the most violent music she could remember, careless of what she was giving away, her whole being so suffused with outrage that she could have burst with it.

Eventually the wild torrent of emotion died away into grey resignation. Instead of behaving like an adult she had lost her temper and stamped around, indulging in her first tantrum since childhood.

Leo must be wretched; Grace's test results would have been a blow. Her heart ached. She would, she decided, give him time to simmer down, and then she'd go and tell him how sorry she was. She was sitting quietly, idly doodling with a handful of notes, when she heard the sound of an engine. For a moment she thought it was the launch, but its rapidly increasing loudness gave the lie to that. The sea-plane was circling the bay prior to landing. Footsteps sounded outside; she heard Frankie's voice.

Tansy half got to her feet, then subsided back on to the stool. She was not one of the family; it wasn't her place to go out and see who was arriving.

Her back straightened; she turned her head away from the tantalising glimpse of the sea through the French windows and began to play in earnest, choosing one of Rachmaninov's concertos, all fire and flash and loud chords, using the music as a shield.

A wrenched scream stopped her hands as if she'd been pole-axed. Heart thudding, she raced through the door and out on to the terrace, skidding to a halt when she realised who was standing out on the terrace.

Rick. An embarrassed Rick, with his mother clinging to him and weeping as though her heart had broken. He was awkwardly patting her back, until he saw Tansy erupt through the door. Then his expression became filled with such astonishment that she had to laugh even though her stupid heart was cracking.

Now that Rick was here she didn't have to stay. She could go.

And she realised, as she turned away and went into the kitchen to make tea for them all, now, when it was too late, she realised she didn't really want to.

She wanted to be with Leo. Oh, not like this, not a pawn to be moved around, but an equal. She wanted Leo to look at her and see her, Tansy Ormerod, as the woman more essential to him than the breath he drew and the water he drank.

If that was love, it seemed she was in love with the swine. A life-saving numbness saved her from breaking down and beating the bench with her fists, but that wasn't going to last. Eventually the pain would cut through, and by then she wanted to be out of this house and back in Wellington, as far away from Leo as possible.

She poured boiling water into the teapot, listening to the sound of Leo's voice as he brought some sort of order to the scene out on the terrace. Her heart contracted. No, of course she wasn't in love with him. Attraction was different from love, a purely physical need based on hormones, and right from the start she'd recognised she was attracted to Leo. This empty ache was simply frustration.

Grace was still weeping when Tansy brought the tray on to the terrace; Frankie was dabbing her eyes awkwardly, and poor Rick still looked mortally embarrassed, but, she realised after one long, intent glance, also serene and purposeful and adult, as though he had grown up in the four months he'd been away. Physically he was much improved, being tanned and lean with muscles that told their own story of hard work.

Both he and Leo got to their feet when she came out; Leo took the tray from her with a curt, 'Thank you,' and set it down on the table.

'Where are you going?' he asked as she turned.

She gave him a cool, considering stare. 'To my room.'

His brows drew together in a black frown, but after a moment he said curtly, 'Very well.'

Tansy walked stiffly off and sat down with the music she had written the night before. However, she couldn't concentrate, and when she forced it, she looked at the pages with sheer indifference, feeling none of the usual pleasure and pain. Sheer terror fountained through her. If Leo had set up a barrier between her and the only thing that really mattered, she would never forgive him.

Afterwards she had no idea how long she sat there willing herself to experience some sort of emotion. A tap at the door on to the terrace was a relief. Rick hovered, looking both pleased and anxious.

'Come in,' she said, leaping up to hug him, because although he was the indirect cause of all her worries, she was glad to see him. 'You look good! Four months has made a big difference.'

'Hard work and lots of food.' He returned her hug with interest, strong arms holding her tightly for a moment.

She stepped back, surveying his face. The biggest changes had been internal ones. This was a young man, not a strung-out, terrified boy. 'So, how are things?'

'Pretty well. I'm going to be all right. We did a lot of talking, a lot of discussion, and I've worked out what I'm going to do.'

'And what's that?'

He looked peaceful, yet excited. 'I'm going to be a minister,' he said, enjoying the play of expression across her face.

'A *minister*? As in the church?' She collapsed into her chair, staring at him with wide, wondering eyes.

He grinned. 'Yes. I've always wanted to be, I've always felt that God was calling me, but I was too weak. I wanted to be like Leo, to be big and macho and have everyone look up to me and respect me and envy me. Boarding-school isn't a terribly good place to be different in, you know, and I think that's why I was stupid enough to try drugs. It made me feel good and in control, for a while, anyway.'

She looked steadily at him. It seemed too facile, too easy, and yet there was no shadow in the blue eyes, no hesitation. She sensed an inner strength that hadn't been there before. Rick had discovered himself; he was no longer at war with his soul.

Relief sharpened her voice. 'So that's it, then.'

'Yeah.' He sat down on the edge of the bed and leaned forward, saying earnestly, 'It was you, you know, who made me see it. You didn't preach, you weren't shocked or superior, and you didn't think taking drugs was romantic or wicked or anything but stupid.'

'Did I say that?' she asked.

'No, you didn't judge me at all, but I could tell. You're so focused, so sure about your life, so prepared to give up everything for your ambition, that it made me realise just how weak I'd been, how I'd thrown away all the advantages I have because I wasn't prepared to accept myself as I was. I realised there could be pleasure in poverty, that life is what we make of it rather than what it does to us. I owe you a lot, Tansy. If it hadn't been for you I'd probably have gone on downhill and heaven knows where I'd have ended up.'

'I doubt that very much,' she said robustly. 'You were the one who wanted to go to the camp, and who stuck it out. You pulled yourself back up, not me.'

He said seriously, 'It was the best thing I ever did. Boy, they were tough. They sort of made us strip ourselves down to nothing, and then rebuild, brick by painful brick. It was shattering and I didn't want to do it, because I didn't like what I saw, but one thing about the camp, you can't get away!'

'I rang a while ago,' she said.

He lifted his brows. She said discreetly, 'Leo found me, of course, as you guessed he would, and told me that your mother was ill, so I rang to see what I should do. Your leader said not to contact you.'

'I see.' He nodded. 'I wasn't ready,' he said with quiet conviction. 'I'd got over the addiction, but I was still resisting the thought of any sort of vocation. The ministry's such a nerdy career!' He smiled.

'When did you finally give in?'

His smile widened into a grin. 'About a week ago. I was stuck on a cliff halfway up a mountain, and I thought, Oh, what the hell. Here I am, God. You can do whatever you like with me.'

Tansy laughed. 'Just like that?'

'Yeah. Just like that. You've no idea how relieved I was. But that's enough about me. How did you come to be here? I nearly died when I saw you in the doorway. For a minute I thought I was hallucinating!'

Tansy's mouth tightened. She eased away from him and picked up the sheets of paper, holding them and tapping them on the desk to make a neat pile. Without expression, she said, 'Your brother can be very insistent.'

'I know, that's why I made you promise not to tell him where I was. I don't suppose he was very pleased when you refused. By and large, people tend not to refuse Leo anything.'

There was a hint of hero-worship, but none of the old hopeless longing in his tone. He spoke with a tranquil acceptance that finally convinced Tansy he was all right.

'He was angry.' If she told him just what a rat his idolised big brother really was, it would only hurt. In the end she said tonelessly, 'We went out together a few times, and then he suggested I come up for the holidays. I think he felt better keeping an eye on me.'

'Yeah, I'm sure he did.' He might not accept her words at face value, but he wasn't going to press the point. 'Well, I'd better go and see Mum again, I suppose.'

Tansy flicked a look at him. Yes, she thought, noting his smile, Rick was going to be able to deal with his mother. The process of character reconstruction and the relief at making his decision had helped him discover the source of his inner strength.

When Rick had gone she stood looking down at the music, telling herself that it was the best thing she had ever done, that she should be proud of it. It was the truth, but the knowledge didn't work. Oh, she could summon some cool intellectual pride in it, but her heart was shattering, shattering in her breast, because music was no longer enough for her.

She ate lunch by herself. Exhausted by joy, Grace had retired to her bed. Rick was with her, and presumably Leo too. Frankie served Tansy her meal out on the terrace before disappearing. Oddly forlorn, she ate, cleared and washed up, then went for a swim and a long walk before sleeping the rest of the afternoon away on her bed.

It was almost dusk when she woke. Outside the sun was going down, tinting tiny clouds on the horizon with clear, pure gold. Yawning, slightly headachy, she got off the bed and stood looking down at her music. She had to get out of here before her façade cracked and she made a fool of herself.

Leo walked in through the door. Eyes as clear and fathomless as green diamonds searching her face, he said quietly, 'I'd like to persuade you to stay.'

'No.' She didn't even have to think.

'Why?'

'You know damned well why.'

His hard mouth twisted. 'You don't forgive, do you?'

'No, not easily.'

'Very well, then. I'll arrange for you to fly back down to Wellington.'

She said crisply, 'Tomorrow.'

'If that's when you want to go.'

'I do.'

The warm light of afternoon fell over him, outlining him with a rim of gold, burnishing his hair but shadowing his face so that she couldn't see his emotions. He seemed to be keeping himself well in restraint. Why did he need to? After all, he had what he wanted; Rick was back, and she was completely expendable.

She'd be well rid of him.

'Very well,' he said evenly. 'Are you coming along to dinner?'

Reluctantly, because she couldn't think of an excuse, she accompanied him. Up again and aglow, Grace was radiant, her natural tendency to flutter around Rick dispelled a little by the difference in him.

She said, 'I heard you playing this morning, Tansy—absolutely magnificent! Is that sort of music you compose?'

If only! 'I use classical forms,' Tansy told her. 'Symphonies, concerti, that sort of thing.'

Grace nodded. 'It's a vocation, then.'

'Oh, yes.' Rick grinned affectionately at Tansy. 'She's obsessed with music, dedicated to it. It's the most important thing in her life.'

'Truly?' Grace said, intrigued yet disbelieving.

Tansy nodded. 'I'd shrivel up and die if I didn't have it.'

Grace looked taken aback. 'It must be quite a burden,' she said vaguely.

'A great delight, too,' Tansy responded.

Dinner was an odd meal; Grace was so happy, yet her delight in her son's return was qualified by a puzzled frustration as she realised that something had caused a fundamental change in him.

Frankie sat quietly, her shrewd glance lingering on each of them in turn. Rick was doing his best to reduce the last traumatic few months to normality. Tansy ate silently, speaking when she was spoken to, trying to separate herself from them.

Leo too seemed abstracted.

When Tansy at last went to her room she was exhausted. After getting ready for bed she sat down to look at her manuscript. It took her half an hour of searching, three or four times around the room and out on the terrace, to convince her that the music she had written at Taupo and again last night was not there.

No errant breeze had tossed it across lawn and trees. Someone had come into her room, removed the sheets from under the hairbrush where she'd left them anchored, and taken them away. She suddenly realised who it had to be.

Leo. But why?

Sheer fury, spitting white-hot temper so violent that there was nothing she could do to contain it, zig-zagged through Tansy. Before she had a chance to calm down she stormed down the terrace to Leo's room. He was standing in the doorway, looking out across the sea, but he turned his head to watch her progress down the terrace; there was no emotion on the angular features, no warmth in the clear, cold eyes.

Behind him a single lamp spilled a pool of light on to a wide double bed turned down to reveal crisp white sheets. Tansy saw all of this and none of it; her eyes were blazing into Leo's, the last shred of control torn to tatters, fists clenching and unclenching at her sides as she pushed past and stood in the middle of the room, her eyes darting around the room.

'What the hell,' she demanded, 'have you done with my music? What are you up to now?'

He said sharply, 'Quieten down!'

'I mean it; they are the best things I've ever done, and if you've touched them I'll kill you.' She knew she was shouting, knew that others might hear her, but she was past caring.

'It's all right, I tell you.' Lean strong hands slammed the French windows, shutting out the velvet darkness, the soft sounds of the sea on the white beach.

'What have you done with it?' She didn't realise she was wringing her hands together until he caught them in his.

'The hairbrush was not enough to weigh the papers down, because they were blowing through the window when I walked down the terrace,' he said calmly, holding her hands against his heart. 'You weren't around, so I collected them up and brought them here. Then Grace wanted to see me. I've only just got back from talking to her.'

She stared at him, wide, catlike eyes glowing golden in the lamplight, her white face sharp and taut. 'Where are they?' she said fiercely.

'Over there under the book on my dressing-table.'

Tansy snatched the sheets up and skimmed quickly through them, her grip only relaxing when she was satisfied that every one was there.

'Thank you,' she muttered, turning around.

Smiling cynically, he took the music from her and put it back on the table, then pulled her into his arms. 'Don't you trust anyone, Tansy?' he asked before his mouth closed over hers and he kissed her.

Perhaps it was the relief, or the fury that had preceded it, perhaps the hunger that had been building inside her ever since she had seen him. Perhaps it was his potent male appeal, the aura of latent sexuality about him that she responded to. Whatever, when his demanding mouth touched hers she went up like a bushfire in high summer heat, the flames licking through her with such ferocity that she couldn't have resisted even if she'd wanted to.

And she didn't want to. Although it was only making the situation worse, she knew that if she didn't do this she was going to regret it for the rest of her life.

He kissed her with a famished passion, his mouth taking all that she had to give. There was no gentleness, no hesitancy; he was an experienced man driven beyond the strictures of politeness or consideration.

And Tansy gloried in it, giving him everything he wanted, taking what she wanted from him, her hands clasping his broad shoulders with strong, imperative fingers. He tasted like heaven, like sun and sea and excitement, the satisfaction of her most secret needs.

'Tansy,' he said, his voice deep and rough-textured, raw with passion. 'I've wanted this ever since I saw you standing in your black scarecrow clothes singing songs about love and desire and pain with your smoky voice. You looked like a tigress, dangerous and wild, locked in a zoo instead of roaming through jungles. And when the wind threw your beret off and your incredible hair sprang out around your head, I knew I was going to eat my heart out for you. You've driven me mad, for days and weeks...'

His lips on her throat detonated tingles of sensation through her bloodstream, stars exploding in pulse points and pleasure spots, a galaxy of fireworks inside her, heated and swift and all-consuming.

'I knew your skin would feel like ivory satin,' he muttered, 'like silk, like flower petals, smooth and warm and scented. That's what I remember when you're not

with me, your scent, and the golden flames in your eyes,
and that mouth, so controlled I keep wondering what it
would do to me when the control slipped.'

She could have cried out in protest when he pulled
back, reimposing the curb of will over his emotions, and
traced her throbbing mouth with his thumb. 'It's like
heaven,' he said, eerily echoing her thoughts. 'Like
crushed roses dipped in wine, perfumed, intoxicating.'

That probing thumb touched the tip of her tongue,
ran along the serrations of her teeth, and caressed her
lips. She wanted to close her eyes, because it was too
dangerous looking at his; she was engulfed by the purest
green, dragged into a world where the sun was green and
gold, where heat and fire and emotion were inextricably
mixed.

'Tell me what you want,' he commanded.

Eyes dilating endlessly, she shook her head.

His mouth tightened. 'All right,' he said quietly, 'I'll
tell you what I want. Some day, when you trust me, you
might be able to reciprocate.'

'And what do you want?' Was that her voice, dazed
and wondering?

'You,' he said uncompromisingly. 'I want all of you,
everything you have to give, everything I can take, all
of it.'

For a moment fear held her paralysed. She knew then
that if she made love with him she would never be the
same again. Beyond the mere physical fact of surren-
dering her virginity was the even more symbolic acceptance and surrender, the yielding of herself to his male
domination.

Once she had given herself, her world would need to
be reassessed. All of her life Tansy had been an outsider.
She had learned to rely only on herself, had vowed never
to give up control to anyone else. Making love would
shatter that sense of invulnerability.

'All right,' she said, her hand cupping his strong jaw. 'I want that too; everything you have to give, all of you.'

It was an impossible fantasy, of course; he might take his fill of her body, but there were areas of her life he would never touch. And although she would lose herself in his lovemaking, his life and his future held no place for her.

But for tonight they would both pretend.

He made a rough noise in his throat. Tansy's forefinger came to rest on the hollow there, savouring the rapid, fierce pulse beneath her finger. He was so self-sufficient and yet she had done this to him.

'Yes,' he said, and laughed. 'You like power, don't you? So do I, Tansy. Let's see who has the most, shall we?'

She was wearing a peach cotton nightdress with little buttons down the front between pintucks. He slid the buttons open, his eyes never leaving her face, his fingers sure and deft. Tansy looked down, watching fingers barbarically copper against the pale material and the warm glowing cream of her skin.

Fire pooled in the pit of her stomach, streaked through her veins. She had never felt so small, yet she could hear the quick rasp of his breathing, see the hammer of his pulse in his throat, and knew that he was equally excited.

He spread the neckline of the nightgown, looking at the clear skin beneath, the curves of her breasts, and then picked her up and tossed her on to the bed, somehow in the process stripping the little gown from her, so that she landed naked on her back, arms outstretched to protect herself from the sudden thump. Although the mattress was comfortable the contact was abrupt enough to take her breath away for a second.

She didn't know what to expect. She didn't know how to deal with this feeling, this position, lying without clothes under his eyes, tingling with the heated flush of arousal and embarrassment as he looked her over.

'You are so beautiful,' he said, but absently, as though the words had no thought to them, were a pure reaction. He hadn't changed; he still wore well-cut trousers and shirt that made the most of his magnificent body.

Heat began to build in Tansy; a flaunting, taunting need held her in its shameless embrace. Her self-consciousness died, replaced by a fluid languor that seeped like honey into her bones, bringing its own sweet fire. She stretched against the white sheets, acutely conscious of the scent of sunlight in them, fragrant background to the other scents, commingled and exotic, of aroused male and female.

His fingers shook as he pulled off his shirt and shed the rest of his clothes, moving with the prowling sensuality that made him stand out among other men.

Oh, God, she thought, swallowing frantically to ease her dry throat. He was so big...

What followed was like some erotic dream. With him, under his expert tutelage, she was Circe and Cleopatra, Helen of Troy and Venus, all the women who had ever lived and found ecstasy in the arms of their lovers.

She had thought him calculating; he showed her that there was value in restraint, that a slow seduction could heighten desire to an unbearable pitch. She knew him to be experienced; he taught her that knowledge is power.

He stroked down her side and across her stomach with long even movements of his hands that left her quivering and tense, afraid and yet eager. Turning her head into his chest, she found pathways through the haze of curly hair, and found that this, too, added to her anticipation, especially when his abrupt indrawn breath revealed how much he liked her hands on him.

But when at last he bent his charcoal head and took the budding, dusky apricot nipple in his mouth, she cried out, and her hand clenched against him, fingernails digging in. Sensation like hot wires streaked through her.

He laughed beneath his breath. 'I knew you'd be responsive. I knew it...' And he began to suckle, drawing the crest into his mouth, setting up a rhythm that steadied the runaway sensations in her body into an irresistible, uncontainable force, driving her on along a preordained path.

His hand slid down to the tangle of red between her legs; an unmanageable reflex arched her body into a bow as she tried to coax something else from him, to persuade that knowing hand further.

He began to press against the cleft in the same rhythm, and the unknown force within her increased tenfold. Hips moving in a response as old as time, her hand fell away from his chest to rest tensely on the sheets, closing and unclosing as the honeyed fire swept through her, robbing her of strength yet urging her ever onwards.

His scent filled her nostrils; his taste lingered in her mouth, his hand held her prisoner, and all the time he was bringing her closer and closer to some arcane destination.

When the muscles across her stomach and deep within contracted, Tansy called out his name in a thin, high voice.

Lifting his head, he said, 'Yes? Tell me now what you want, Tansy.'

'I don't——' She thrust upwards, trying to find some relief from the throbbing demands of her body.

The swift, involuntary movement brought them together, chest to chest, his thighs between hers. She whimpered, nuzzling him, tugging with eager hands at his hips. Blinded by passion, beyond thought, she only knew that she wanted—needed—him on her and in her.

'Yes,' he said in a harsh, impeded voice, and in one steady stroke completed the joining of their bodies.

Tansy cried out again. For a moment she was transfixed by an intolerable stretching, a feeling of being taken over. Her hands fastened on to his shoulders, felt the fierce flexion of the muscles and sinews; dimly she was aware of his rough breathing.

Then he withdrew, and slowly, smoothly, the invasion receded, and the emptiness was far worse, it left her cold, it left her sobbing with hunger.

'No!' she said wildly.

Again he laughed, and began to set a rhythm, moving with ever-increasing strength. After a few attempts Tansy got her responses under control; her hips accepted him, opposed him; the inner muscles gripped, trying to hold him there.

'Say my name,' he muttered.

Tansy lifted weighted eyelids. He looked different, the darkly flushed skin of his face stretched over a framework suddenly far more prominent than it had ever been before.

'Leo,' she said in a tight voice. 'Leo, oh, God, Leo...'

As though the sound of her voice was an incantation he began to drive deep and savagely into her, forcing her from peak to peak of rapture, conquering everything but her wild need to find out where she was going.

Hair wild around her wild face, eyes suddenly blazing, lips red and generous against heated skin, she stared into his face, caught up by the consuming, primeval inevitability, knowing that just beyond, just a little further on, there was a place that was theirs alone.

And then she found it, a piercing level of sensation, rapture that spread at first like tidal waves, gently inexorable, then crested into summits of pounding, tumultuous exhilaration. She gave a choked cry and lost herself in the ecstasy.

Later, as it was ebbing, Leo found that same destination, the source of all delight, and she watched with slumbrous eyes as passion vanquished him.

A friend had once described lovemaking as life's most consummate sensation; then, Tansy had argued, but now she knew she'd been right. Yet the pleasure that wrapped her in its silken cloak when Leo lay quiet, heavy and infinitely precious on her, was just as intense.

After long moments he rolled over on to his back beside her. Tansy's breath and pulses subsided into normality; the warmth and exultation seeped away, leaving her empty and drained. It didn't help that her friend had told her about this, too; post-coital depression, she'd called it. An ugly term for a grey logic that was reminding Tansy of all the reasons why she should have made sure this hadn't happened.

She said uncertainly, 'I'd better go back.'

'Yes, I suppose you had.'

She didn't want him to say that. She wanted him to ask her to stay, to tell her that she was spending the whole night with him, but of course he was right.

However, when she began to get out of the bed he turned and pulled her close to him, holding her hard against him. Unfuelled by passion, this close, intimate enfolding was almost shocking. She burrowed into his chest, sensing a violence in him that had been there all evening.

'I'd like to think you trust me,' he said against the top of her head, 'but I suppose that's too much to hope for. You're still going back to Wellington?'

She nodded.

He laughed, a grim sound in the quiet air. 'I see. Don't forget me, will you?'

How could she tell him that he was engraved in her heart forever?

She said gruffly, 'No, I won't forget.'

Clutching her music, she walked silently and swiftly back to her room through a night warm and summer-scented, made lyrical by the soft hush of waves on the white sand.

Tansy woke to the sound of the sea, an aching body and an unquiet mind. Yet she didn't regret the previous night.

She had wanted Leo to take her, and she had expected the kind of forthright hunger he'd shown, because that was how she felt, as though nothing in this earth mattered as much as making love with Leo.

No, she didn't regret it. But she shouldn't have done it, just the same. If this enforced stay at the island had done anything, it had shown her just how impossible it was for her world and Leo's to combine. Even if she loved him—and she didn't, because love entailed being prepared to make sacrifices, and she wasn't—and even if he loved her—and that word hadn't crossed his lips— she wouldn't marry him. They had nothing in common.

It hurt to think of leaving the island, of never seeing him again. In his way he was as spoiled as Rick; he behaved with the careless arrogance of a man who had been brought up to believe that he should have his own way. He lived in a world as alien to her as life on Mars would be. She had listened while Grace told her of parties to celebrate the launching of a new wine, of family and friends who went to London to see a show and visit friends and flew back a week later, of holidays spent on a friend's private island in the Fiji group.

Leo had made his own way—he worked very hard and he was going to be famous and rich on his own efforts— but Grace's world was his world too.

Tansy knew what her life was going to be, and she knew what happened to many talented women who married and had children. Love, family life, drained their creative energy from them, held them fast in velvet shackles, and, unless they were ruthless enough to sacrifice children and husband, their talents withered.

Tansy had no intention of sacrificing anyone but herself. Yet in spite of the promptings of common sense she found her breath coming quickly as more potent memories took over her mind. Sternly banishing them, she showered and dressed, girding herself for the inevitable embarrassment of facing him over the breakfast-table.

He wasn't there.

'He went off in the amphibian early this morning,' Rick said absently, eating fish and potato cakes with awe-inspiring enthusiasm. 'It's funny that you didn't hear it, although he left at the crack of dawn. He said he'd be back by eleven o'clock.'

Tansy felt as though she'd been hit in the face. Why hadn't he taken her? Suspicion dug two little lines between her thin brows. What was Leo up to now?

She lifted several large, glowing strawberries on to her cereal and poured yoghurt over the top. Last night he had made her look at herself with new eyes, as a desirable woman, one who could make him almost lose the cool self-containment that was such a part of him. She had never esteemed her body or her face before; he had set a value on them, on her, and she would always remember that once Leo Dacre had wanted her.

There was no future for them, but her suspicion was tempered by a nascent, unbidden hope.

'That's a singularly smug little smile,' Rick observed.

Colour stained the skin above her cheekbones. She chewed a mouthful of cereal and strawberries and remained silent.

'Oh, all right, don't tell me,' he said calmly. 'I'll find out.'

He might, too, if she stayed around long enough. Only she wasn't staying. It would be dangerous; she would become too dependent on Leo, too hungry for his passion, and she had few defences against this unwanted hope.

Breakfast over, she went back to her room, but there was nothing to do there. Rick was sitting with his mother out on the terrace, and something about the set of Grace's shoulders told Tansy she wouldn't be welcome. So she had a swim, showered the salt from her hair, then walked along the beach, fighting a restlessness that came from a deep, underlying pain, one she wouldn't let herself examine or even acknowledge.

Leo was sitting on the terrace with the others when she came back. The glowing bougainvillaea flowers cast dancing shadows over his face, but although he got to his feet when she arrived there was nothing but cold composure to be read in his face, as though the night before had never happened.

'Ricky's just been telling us how you took him in,' he said, when he had seated her.

Tansy sent a swift look at the younger man. Rick grinned. 'She scooped me up from the railway station,' he said cheerfully, 'bought me a hamburger, asked me where I was going to stay the night, and when I stuttered and lied she took me home. Actually, she saved me from a fate worse than death.'

Grace and Frankie stared at him. Tansy was watching Leo; she saw his hand close into a fist, then deliberately relax, the long fingers loose and lax.

'What do you mean?' Grace asked uncertainly.

Tansy directed a narrow-eyed, minatory glare Rick's way. 'He certainly doesn't——'

'Come on, Tansy,' Rick interrupted. 'I meant just what I said. There are two ways of making enough money to live if you're on the streets. One is to steal. The other is prostitution. And sometimes you don't have the choice.'

'That's enough.' Leo's voice was hard.

Rick shook his head. 'Sorry, but it's not. Tansy took me in and fed me when she hardly had enough money to feed herself. She put up with me when I wanted drugs, and even let me stay after I'd stolen money from her to get them.'

Tansy's head turned; clearly Grace now knew about Rick's experiments with drugs, but she looked sick at this, and her graceful hands writhed in her lap.

'She saved my life,' Rick said gruffly, 'because if I'd had to use either of the other alternatives I think I'd have killed myself.'

A small protesting noise from Grace was drowned by Leo's harsh voice. 'Ricky, you're upsetting your mother.'

'I'm sorry for that, but I think you should all know what Tansy did for me.' He reached over and took his mother's hand, but continued firmly, 'She gave me a breathing space, and when I pinched the money from her it made me feel so disgusted that I finally faced what I was doing to myself. I realised that I had to get myself together, and I knew where I wanted to do it. I borrowed the money from Tansy to get to the South Island; she trusted me to use it to get there and not spend it on dope, so I did.'

He looked defiantly at his brother. 'And I made her promise not to tell you where I was.'

'Why? You make me sound like an ogre, whereas all I had in mind was a good therapist——'

Rick smiled crookedly. 'I know. With you and Mother watching over my shoulder.'

Leo said nothing, his expression aloof. Only the golden glitter in the depths of his eyes revealed the emotions that lurked there.

'I wanted to do it on my own,' Rick said reasonably. 'You guys go for the people with credentials, letters after their names, but Mitch's got nothing like that, just a desire to help people like me and a conviction that hard work and no bullshit can do it. It works. We busted our guts down there, and when we were completely exhausted we sat around and talked. Man, he was tough! None of this "My mother smacked me once on the leg so I'm too fragile to cope with this rotten world"! Mitch didn't take any rubbish. He told us right from the start that in this world we're born alone, we live alone and we die alone. In a hundred years' time no one's going to remember us. What we do is up to us entirely, because we make our own lives. And if we OD out of it, we've just wasted the world's resources.'

'He sounds horrible!' Grace said indignantly.

'Well, he doesn't come over as filled with the milk of human kindness,' Rick said drily, 'but believe me, he stopped the self-pity—what little I had left after Tansy dealt to me.'

Grace looked across at Tansy, her expression very illuminating. Half of her was pleased that Tansy had been there for Rick, and the other half was almost resentful. Tansy understood; it must be shattering for the older woman to realise that when he most needed help her son had fled from her.

Leo was leaning back, his face impassive, his eyes hidden under half-closed lids. After one swift glance Tansy kept her eyes on Rick's earnest face.

He continued, 'Well, once the self-pity was out of the way, we were able to find out for ourselves just why we'd let ourselves get into such a state. And that was a no-holds-barred experience, I can tell you. It was probably the most humiliating thing I'll ever have to go through.'

Grace looked indignant all over again. 'But why?' she asked. 'What *had* happened to you? Where did we go wrong?'

'You didn't,' he said promptly. 'I did. I was too weak to understand that I couldn't keep up with Leo, and too self-centred to do anything about it, so I blamed him, and you, and school and society and God for everything that went wrong, instead of accepting that it was up to me. I thought the world owed me a whole lot of things I wasn't getting, like respect and admiration and esteem, without realising that those things don't come to you just because of who you are. You have to earn them.'

There was an odd little silence. Grace sat for a moment with her mouth half open, her eyes darting uncertainly from her son to Leo's impassive face, then back again.

'I was ready to believe it,' Rick said, his mouth curving slightly at the corners as he glanced from one to the other, 'because I'd lived with Tansy for those couple of months. She started off with nothing, and she's worked like stink to get where she is. She doesn't ask anything from anybody, she just sets her sights and keeps going until she's got there.'

Colour heated Tansy's cheeks. Troubled by the full weight of their attention, she said lightly, 'It helps when you're single-minded.'

'Perhaps. I know you've dedicated your life to your music; that's the sort of dedication I want. I've never admired anyone as much as I admire you.'

Not the kindest remark he could have made, especially not with that sincerity ringing in his voice and shining in his eyes. Grace said rigidly, 'Well, I'm very grateful you were there, Tansy, but Ricky, surely you could have told us?'

He squeezed her hand. 'I was ashamed. And I had to do it on my own,' he explained. 'Tansy took off on her own when she had to, and I needed to do this, to prove that I could. It was a test.'

'But——'

Leo's voice overrode Grace's plaintive one. 'You may not have had a very good opinion of yourself,' he said, 'and we may have treated you like a child long after you had stopped being one, but I think you've proved to everyone, and especially to yourself, that you're well and truly grown up now.'

Rick flushed, his expression revealing just how much this meant to him. 'Thanks,' he said quietly.

CHAPTER EIGHT

IT WAS a strangely touching moment. Feeling that they needed to be alone Tansy got to her feet, but Leo followed suit, saying remotely, 'You'll have to excuse us. Tansy and I have a couple of things to discuss.'

Dwarfed by his size, Tansy walked away with him. She knew what he was going to say; she might as well say it herself. As soon as they reached his office she said without preamble, 'You told me I could leave today.'

'I'm sorry,' he said coldly. His face was uncompromising, the strong bone-structure harshly emphasised, his eyes guarded and unreadable. 'I got a call early this morning—I had to go to Auckland to interview a man who quite possibly killed his wife. Will tomorrow do? I'll drive you down and put you on a plane.'

'The bus will do,' she said, traumatised by a sudden, wrenching pain. An utterly ridiculous pain; apart from sex they had nothing in common, so why did she feel that sense of bitter betrayal?

He lifted his brows, as though the very idea of a bus was absurd. 'I'll put you on a plane,' he said, calm word following calm word.

Yet he was angry. She could feel it pulsing him through him in dark waves.

'I don't want to cost you any more than I have to,' she said scornfully.

'No, that's fairly obvious. You've made your point, you know, with all the subtlety of a sledgehammer. I've become heartily sick of those few clothes you deign to wear.'

163

So he had noticed. She didn't bother to hide a smile of totally feline malice. 'Sorry, I don't wear clothes to appeal to men.'

'You don't,' he said courteously, 'wear clothes to attract anything except moths and sympathy.'

Tansy's temper surfaced with a rush of blood to the head. 'You didn't seem to worry last night.'

'Last night all I could think of was making love to you,' he said brutally. 'And you wanted it, Tansy. Remember that, when you start feeling righteous and smug. I may have no place in your life, but when you called my name in my arms I was the centre of your world.'

She turned and left, because he was right.

Like her he was eager to be gone; they said their goodbyes the night before, Tansy promising to keep in touch with Rick, and left the island with the rising sun at their backs and gulls calling over a sea the tender grey of a dove's breast.

Apart from her guitar and her bag and the clothes she had on, Tansy took nothing from the island. Until she got home she had to wear the T-shirt and jeans Leo had bought, but as soon as she was back in Wellington he'd get them back.

Neither spoke in the car; Tansy pretended to be asleep. She was grappling with a set of emotions so turbulent and novel that she couldn't make sense of them, especially the aching emptiness that threatened to swamp her.

She sat up abruptly when, instead of heading straight to Auckland, Leo turned the car off at the Riverhead junction. She demanded fiercely, 'Where are we going?'

'I thought you might like to see your parents before you leave Auckland.'

'No!' The word burst out from her before she had time to think, and with it came pain and guilt and a sly shame, because she didn't want him to know her foster-parents, and she certainly didn't want them to see her with Leo.

'Why not?'

She gnawed her lip, thinking furiously. Damn it, she wasn't ashamed of them! They were good people; it hadn't been their fault she'd been an interloper. Her main function in life, she thought bitterly. 'Because I don't,' she said stubbornly at last.

'Tough.'

Her fiery glance traced a profile autocratically carved in copper. She looked away and said in a stifled voice, 'I won't tell you where they live.'

'I know where they live,' he said. 'Tansy, calm down. It won't hurt you to say hello to them.'

She said caustically, 'Don't you think you've interfered with my life enough?'

His jaw hardened. 'This will be the last time,' he said casually.

The house looked the same. Beds of petunias glowed brazenly in the sun beneath standard roses with bold, brilliant flowers.

Ignoring Leo, Tansy opened her door, got out, and stalked through the gate and up the path.

The curtains had been changed. These ones were airy net with a design in yellow and green. Tansy thought she should feel something beyond this awful emptiness.

She knocked. Almost immediately, the door swung open. 'Yes?' Pam O'Brien asked. Skimming past Tansy, her eyes widened when they reached Leo. Pam's free hand patted back a lock of hair as she smiled uncertainly at him.

Just as well, Tansy thought with a flash of irritation, she wasn't expecting the prodigal daughter routine. 'Hello, Mum,' she said laconically.

She saw the moment her adoptive mother recognised her. A familiar wariness and irritation crept into the fine eyes. 'Sherryl,' Pam said, holding the door like a shield. 'What are you doing in Auckland?'

'I had to come up.'

'Oh.'

She looked at Leo, who said pleasantly, 'I'm Leo Dacre, Mrs O'Brien, a friend of Tansy's. She's been staying at our place and before she went back to Wellington she wanted to come and see you.' He gave her the million-watt smile.

It had its usual effect. 'Oh,' Pam said again, looking both dazzled and bewildered.

Taking pity on her, Tansy said, 'We can only stay for a short time. I have to go back to Wellington today.'

'Well—you'd better come on in, then.'

As always, the house was immaculate, from the collections of bells and kittens and china thimbles, to the silk flowers on the big new television, and the picture of the thatched cottage embowered in roses of an improbable hue on the wall.

'Would you like a cup of tea?' Pam asked, talking fast and nervously as she put the kettle on. 'Les and Jason and Brett got up before it was light and went fishing off the mouth of the Wade River, but they should be back soon, they weren't going to stay long; Les's going to cut the lawns. Brett's the boy Michelle's engaged to. He's an Australian. Did I tell you in my last letter that we were thinking of shifting to Australia?'

'No, you didn't.' Acutely aware of the way her mother kept darting appreciative little looks at Leo, Tansy couldn't stop her voice from sounding stiff and awkward.

'Well, Brett and Michelle are getting married in May, and they're going to live in Brisbane. Brett says he can get Jason a good job in his father's contracting business, and Les too.'

'Does Dad want to go?'

'Not all that much, but he doesn't like being on the dole.'

'Why is he on the dole?'

Pam flushed. 'Didn't I tell you he was made redundant at Flaxman's?'

They both knew she hadn't. Tansy said peaceably, 'I must have forgotten.'

'Well, anyway, it's hard for a man his age to get a job here, but Brett says he'd have no trouble in Queensland.' Pam poured boiling water into the pot and set cups and saucers out on the bench, her hands moving deftly. She went across to the fridge and extracted a jug of milk. 'And it's not as though there's anything to keep us here,' she said, and immediately looked embarrassed.

Tansy wasn't upset. She didn't blame Pam for not considering her a part of the family.

'What do you do, Mr Dacre?' Pam said quickly. 'Are you from Wellington, too?'

'No, I live in Auckland. I'm a barrister,' he said.

'Oh, a lawyer.' Pam glanced swiftly from Leo's handsome face to Tansy's, her speculation plain as she poured milk into the cups and opened a packet of biscuits.

'I'm not hungry,' Tansy said quickly.

Pam said, 'You look as though you could do with a good meal. Aren't you eating properly?' and buttered a couple of crispbreads, putting tomato and processed cheese on them.

They sat down on the chintz sofa. 'Have you been on holiday?' Pam asked.

Tansy nodded. 'Further north. I——'

'Oh, there are the others.' With what was certainly relief Pam got to her feet as a car rolled in behind the house with a neat little dayboat on a trailer behind. 'It's Les's pride and joy, that boat,' she confided.

Tansy and Leo left half an hour later, Tansy wondering whether she was as relieved at her departure as they were, or saddened because they had grown so far apart. When she had left the waters had closed over her place, leaving no sign that she had ever been there.

Leo, on the other hand, had been a great success. At first her father and Jason and Brett, a tall, laconic Australian of few words, had viewed him with suspicion, but the potent charm worked just as well with men as it did with women. Within a very few minutes they were discussing New Zealand's rugby team and its chances in the next season. When it was time to go they all seemed rather sorry to see him leave.

Tansy brooded over this all the way out to the airport, wondering in a self-pitying way whether she was doomed to be the outsider all her life.

'How much did Rick steal off you?' he asked abruptly as he switched off the engine outside the domestic terminal.

She had expected it and had her answer ready. 'That's between him and me,' she said. 'He'll pay me one day.'

'Don't you need the money now?'

'I'll manage.'

She was glad to get out of the car. 'Don't bother to come in with me,' she said in a crisp voice.

'Tansy, stop pushing,' he returned curtly.

Apparently supremely unconscious of the gazes from passers-by that lingered so interestedly on his face and the width of his shoulders, he checked her in.

'So, goodbye,' he said when the official bits were over.

She swallowed and said steadily, 'Goodbye.'

'Try not to hate me,' he said, his mouth twisting on the words.

She lifted surprised eyes. 'No—I mean, I don't.'

The smile became even more lop-sided. 'I can always tell when you lie. Take care, Tansy.'

She said, 'You too,' and turned and walked briskly away from him and on to the plane.

There, she stared blindly at the panorama of New Zealand's wildly varying countryside until she sank into an oblivious lethargy that lasted until they landed.

Typically, Wellington turned on a chilly, damp afternoon. Or perhaps, Tansy thought, she carried her own personal weather around with her. The flat was cold and damp and smelt of mould; dust lay thick over the furniture.

Wrinkling her nose at the smell of neglect and stale food, she cleared the little fridge out, washed her clothes and changed the sheets, before collapsing into the bed. She didn't sleep, but she was up quite early the next morning and went out with her guitar and busked until late in the afternoon in the Christmas crowds. She had to try to recoup her losses.

Besides, it gave her something to do, something to think about. Only a few days till Christmas, and after that the city would be dead. Still, for the moment the money was good. It was when she went to put it in the bank that she discovered that a large sum, enough to cover her fees for the year and then some, had been deposited in her account.

She asked for the name of the account it had come from, and was told that it had been deposited in cash. 'How would I go about discovering the account number of another person?' she asked.

The teller looked at her. 'We can't give you that information, I'm afraid,' she said.

'Then how did this get into mine?'

The teller looked intrigued. 'If the depositor didn't know your account number they would have had to know your name and possibly your mother's maiden name, as well as your address and the branch.'

All of which Leo knew from his damned dossier. To find out what her bank was he'd only have had to look in her bag. Anger heated a heart she'd thought cold forever. She said, 'Could you find out whether a Mr Leo Dacre of Remuera in Auckland has an account?'

The teller touched the computer, then shook her head. 'I'm sorry, no.'

The classic pay-off, in fact, made with grubby notes for services rendered. Furious, and feeling curiously besmirched, Tansy left the bank. She marched off to the local office of a charity that dealt with drug addicts and donated the whole amount, asking that receipt be made out in Leo's name and sent to the island.

The clothes she had left in the wardrobe and chest of drawers on the island arrived by courier the next day. It hurt to pay the freight, but she sent them straight back along with the ones she'd worn home.

Christmas came in with triumphant weather, hot and breezy, proper summer at last. Tansy spent the holidays alone, intimating vaguely to enquiring friends that she had made other arrangements; it wasn't fair to inflict her moods on anyone else. It seemed easier to treat it as just another day, a blessedly quiet day, free from the constant roar of traffic and the chatter of crowds.

The day after Boxing Day the clothes returned, with a note attached. 'I can keep this up all year', the bold dark blue writing said.

Tansy seethed. She took a savage pleasure in scrawling a note to tell Leo that she had donated the clothes to a very grateful charity shop. On the same day she got a letter from the landlord reminding her that she was to be out of the flat by the end of March.

By New Year she knew she couldn't stay in Wellington, where she had met Leo. It was ridiculous to miss him so much, to go to sleep with his face in her mind's eye, to dream of him, and wake with tears burning in her eyes. It had to be the well-known virgin's fixation on the first man she made love with, because she could not—*would not*—be in love with him.

Defiantly, she decided to go south, to Queenstown, and see how she got on there.

She arrived three days later, dusty and crumpled and hot, but with something like hope in her heart. Surely here, on this magnificent lake, with the mountains around and the splendour that was Otago, she'd find some sort of surcease for the pain that was eating her heart hollow.

Certainly she found holidaymakers. She rented a bed in a youth hostel and discovered in the ever-changing flow of people from all over the world some sort of diversion, if only because she was never alone all that time; she slept in a dormitory, and there was always someone around, usually keen to improve their English.

After a month she realised that she wasn't pregnant. It had been worrying her, and the realisation was a relief, in a way. At least she knew.

She didn't go to work that day. Instead she walked up the hill and found a place beneath the trees that looked out over the lake and the amazing range of mountains, aptly named the Remarkables, that rose so abruptly and steeply from the lakeshore. She sat there for a long time, awed by such beauty, before she realised she was weeping, the tears running silently down her cheeks.

It was time to stop lying to herself. She loved Leo, loved him with an intensity that terrified her. Arrogant and high-handed though he was, arbitrary and ruthless, overbearing and dictatorial—she could lie there all day with the hot blue sky burning above her and the scent of pines in her nostrils and the glittering, chilly waters of the lake dancing below the sombre, steep-sided mountains, and never run out of insults—but she loved him. And she had wanted his child, longed for it, secretly hugged the knowledge that she might be pregnant to her like a prized and precious gift.

She sat there until the sun went down in a glorious ferocity of colour. Then, light-headed with hunger, she walked down to the buzzing little town. During the long day she had come to terms with the impossibility of her love. Her life was dedicated to making music, superb and lasting music; even if there were a possibility of some sort of relationship, Leo would demand more of her than she was prepared to give.

At the end of February she arrived back in Wellington, more fine-drawn in spite of skin slightly gilded by the hot southern sun, without enough money to pay her university fees, and still without any clear idea of how she was going to cope. For the first time in her life she felt lethargic, as though making up her mind was too much trouble. Anything but drifting seemed too difficult to do. She had to force herself to work through the long, tiring days.

This appalling weariness of spirit, and the loss of the autonomy she had always prided herself on, terrified her. Busking didn't help. After the Christmas splurge few people wanted to pay for something they could hear for free. Even if she had earned enough, she wasn't sure that she had the courage or the determination to go on with her master's degree.

Damn Leo Dacre. Loving him was stripping her of her independence and ambition; her whole image of herself was revealed as a lie.

She began actively to pursue the possibility of a scholarship or grant to cover her fees, but nothing eventuated. A cold fear made it hard to concentrate. She began playing all day on the street, even going to the railway station at rush-hour in spite of its rougher clientele.

Late one evening she was walking up the street to her flat when a car slowed and stopped beside her. She didn't need to look to see who drove it; a sudden quickening deep inside told her.

'Tansy,' Leo said.

Her heart squeezed by a giant fist, she looked at him with antagonistic eyes. 'What do you want?'

'I don't want to discuss that here.'

Hope struggled to be born, hope and something she'd thought dead for ever, trust. She nodded and led the way into the flat.

Just inside the door he stopped, asking without expression, 'Are you pregnant?'

She should have known. 'No.'

It hurt fiercely to see the subtle relaxation that indicated his relief. He didn't want her, and he certainly wouldn't want her child. He thought her a common prostitute—ex-prostitute, perhaps, but that didn't alter the stigma.

He said, 'I won't say I'm not pleased.'

Tansy stared stonily at him. 'I'm sure you are,' she said tonelessly.

'Come out to dinner with me.'

'No, thanks.'

The words came without thought. She was not going to be a convenience, eager to warm his bed whenever he came to Wellington. Damn it, she might love him, but she had pride.

'Why not?' he said, his self-possession failing entirely to hide the note of determination in his voice. 'You must realise we have to talk.'

He was watching her with calculation and an intentness that set alarm signals ululating through her. Her only hope was to remain cool, to give him no advantage at all.

'Then we can talk here,' she said quietly. 'Sit down and I'll make some tea. I'm thirsty.'

He lowered himself into the one chair, watching her as she moved around the tiny kitchen, his green eyes disturbing and dangerous. He had lost weight, she was sure. Pouring the hot liquid into two mugs, she felt an overwhelming protectiveness, almost as strong as the bitter sense of betrayal that had been eating at her for weeks.

'So, what do you want to talk about?'

He lifted an eyebrow. 'Why were you so intransigent over the money I tried to give you?' he asked after a tense moment, his eyes piercing as they rested on her face.

'I didn't do anything to earn it,' she said curtly.

'Is that why you left the clothes behind, then gave them to a charity shop?' His voice was cold. 'I didn't think you were so petty, Tansy.'

'I don't wear clothes I haven't paid for.'

His mouth hardened. 'You mean you were making a gesture, showing me just how eager you were to wipe me from your life.'

She shrugged. 'How's Rick?'

He drank the peppermint tea with a faint expression of distaste. 'He's fine. He was right and so were you. We'd been smothering him. I would have had him out of that camp so fast and into a good psychologist's hands—but I was wrong. He needed to prove to himself that he could do it. The whole experience has certainly matured him. It's hard for Grace, but she's learning that if she wants to keep him she has to let him go.'

'Does he still want to go into the church?'

He smiled, but there was something watchful about his gaze. 'Yes. I think it's a true vocation.'

'I'm glad,' she said.

'How is your music coming along?'

'Fine.' She hadn't written anything since the day she had discovered she wasn't going to have Leo's child.

He got up and came across, bending so that she could feel his breath on her lips. His kiss on her cheek was light, almost casual. 'Take care, Tansy, and good luck.'

She watched him go with such anguish gripping her heart that for a moment she thought she might call him back. Still and hunched, she waited until the violent impulse died, and her breath steadied. Then she got up and tipped the tea out, her lips held tightly together to stop them trembling.

At last she understood that for her there would never be another man like him.

The underlying lassitude that had kept her prisoner ever since she left the island wouldn't let her go, but she decided to ignore it. The next day she sat down and let the notes fall off her pen and fit themselves into patterns, writing until she was exhausted and the night had fallen around her. A wild little wind wailed eerily around the sides of the house; she looked out at a sky where harried clouds revealed glimpses of the summer stars in the great bowl of the sky.

And she wept, wept for the wasteland her life had become, wept because there was no happy ending for them.

She had always felt she was cut off from the rest of humanity, that something in her character made her an outcast, unable to fit in. She had made a hash of every relationship she had had. Her birth mother had thought so little of her that she had abandoned her, leaving her to die. The O'Briens had wanted to love her, but had only been able to watch with bewilderment as she repelled their attempts to make her one of the family.

And Leo had made sweet, angry love to her, then walked away from her as though she was nothing but dross.

'Self-pity,' she said out loud, turning away and looking angrily around her little domain. 'The refuge of the weak. And whatever else you are, you are not weak!'

A salutary and very necessary homily, it didn't do anything to ease her grief, but she went to bed stubbornly resolved to carry on without indulging in any more useless recriminations.

A couple of days later she received a note from Professor Paxton asking her to go and see him. Somewhat bewildered, she struggled up the hill and found him in his office.

He had good news. 'Tony Adams rang me the day before yesterday,' he said, beaming at her. 'He went to the recital we did last October, and was very impressed by your work.'

'Who's Tony Adams?'

'The television producer. You know, he does those superb wildlife documentaries.'

Tansy didn't have a television, but she had seen several of the award-winning documentaries at friends' places. 'Oh, yes, of course.'

'You don't sound in the least curious,' he complained. 'He wants you to do the music for his next documentary on the Chatham Islands! Oh, and even better, I've managed to ferret out a grant which will pay for your fees! If you're thrifty you should be able to get through the year without needing to busk.'

'I thought you said——'

He shuffled some papers on his incurably untidy desk and found a sheet. 'Yes, here it is. I've filled it in—just sign it, will you?'

Obediently Tansy signed, but said as he folded it and put in it an envelope, 'Where did it come from?'

'Oh, there are always grants hanging around, it's just a matter of finding them, and being a little creative. Now, about the concert at Easter——'

Tansy tried to be enthusiastic. She thought she fooled Professor Paxton; she almost fooled herself. Had it happened a few months before she'd have been ecstatic, because being commissioned to write music for television was the start of many a career. She could establish a reputation, and take it from there.

The grant was icing on the cake. Very thick icing—in fact, it was astoundingly generous, with a good big lump sum to start off with, so Tansy could afford to buy new clothes. Which, in spite of his cruel gibes about her taste, she bought in the colours Leo had chosen for her, finding some obscure comfort in this small link.

Suddenly her life became very busy. Apart from her studies, the business of fitting music to the documentary was infinitely fascinating, and she enjoyed it very much, just as she enjoyed getting ready for the concert. She hadn't intended to put forward the music she had written after Leo's departure, but Professor Paxton saw it, and, after reading it, insisted.

'You've done some good stuff over the holidays,' he said, clearly pleased and surprised at the amount. 'But I think this is the best. What's it called?'

She shrugged. 'It hasn't got a name.'

'Name it, woman, name it.'

'Oh, call it *Study in G*.'

'Too much like *Air on a G String*. You'll have to come up with something else.'

Over her shoulder she said, 'Well, call it *Requiem for an Unborn Child*.'

He sent her a sharp look, but he didn't pursue the matter, for which Tansy, already regretting her comment, was extremely thankful.

Tony Adams was delighted with her quirky music for the documentary, and the money she received paid her fees for the year. He began to talk about the next series he was doing, and provisionally booked her, if funding could be found. She was contacted by someone else, who asked if she could come up with a signature tune for a new soap opera, and the same executive suggested that she produce for consideration music for a historical serial set in New Zealand's gold rush days.

And from a flyer in her letterbox she found a new flat in another old house a few streets away. This one had been renovated and came with furniture and a separate bedroom for a surprisingly modest rent, so that compared to her old one she was living in luxury.

All in all, things were going very well, better than she could ever have hoped a few months ago. So why did people start recommending that she take multi-vitamins?

While she was actually working she was able to forget Leo, but at all other times his memory taunted her aching heart. So she drove herself relentlessly. Easter came early this year, so she spent long hours rehearsing her requiem with the orchestra. The players were enthusiastic about it and eventually she was almost able to consider it as nothing more than a piece of music.

Almost, because far too often she remembered when it had been composed.

Deciding not to wear her usual conducting outfit—it brought back too many memories of the last time she had worn it—she bought herself a new dress, a severe black silk softened by a swathe of oyster-white satin around the neck that somehow didn't drain the colour and life from her skin.

On the night of the concert she watched nervously as the hall filled. Wellingtonians supported their theatres and small cultural groups with acclaim and enthusiasm; they made a discerning audience. But everything went well. For the first time ever the French horn even managed to arrive on the right beat. As she bowed at the end, Tansy knew from the applause that the audience had enjoyed it. She could feel their pleasure, their interest, but more than that, they told her so afterwards at the small party that always followed the concert.

'Marvellous,' people cooed, kissing her cheek, patting her on the back, hugging her. Many of them meant it.

'A very promising new talent,' a newspaper critic said, lifting his beer glass in a toast. One of the columnists for a weekly magazine was extremely complimentary, promising a good review after he'd spoken to her for a long time about her music.

Tansy supposed she managed to say the right things, although next morning she couldn't remember. It had taken her ages to get to sleep, and she woke heavy-eyed and thick-headed. She went for a walk, trying to analyse her emotions and put them into some sort of order.

Just because she had one piece of music reviewed well didn't mean that the end of her struggle was anywhere near at hand. That music had been ripped from her heart; she still had a long way to go before anyone would accept her as a composer.

But she had her foot on the first rung. Given hard work and luck, and the continued ability to bring forth and shape the music that raged inside her, she'd get there.

Stopping at the top of a sharp incline, she stood looking down over the steep, tumbled land and the houses perched wherever they could find a foothold. Her hands gripped the rail between the footpath and a garden that slid away towards the water. It was one of Wellington's superb autumn days and the harbour lay blue and quiet and brilliant in its enclosure of hills.

Tansy remembered another sea, glittering green and kingfisher-blue around a scattering of islets under a summer sun more hot than any that ever shone here...

Later, she thought she should have known with hidden senses that he was there, but, lost in memories, she was deaf and blind to everything about her.

So when Leo said, 'Why didn't you tell me?' she whirled around. Shock drove the colour from her face. He stood a few feet away, tall and angry. Oh, God, so angry! She could feel it radiating through her, an icy, feral anger that froze the blood in her veins.

'Tell you what?' she asked huskily.

'That you were pregnant. If you'd told me I might have been able to help—make sure that you didn't lose it. But I suppose you were glad.'

The world shifted sideways, sending the hills and the houses tottering. She said, 'What are you talking about?'

He showed his teeth in a snarl. 'God, you really know how to put the screws in. The baby, Tansy, my child. Remember, the one that superbly emotional piece of music you composed and conducted so well last night was named in memory of.'

She shook her head. If she told him the truth it would give too much away—he would know then that she loved him, that she had wanted his child. But nothing had changed. There was still no future for them.

And why, a wicked, vengeful part of her murmured seductively, should he not suffer a little too?

'Was it a miscarriage?' He was white around the lips. 'Or an abortion?'

'No!'

He seemed to relax slightly, but his voice was still arctic. 'I'm glad. Why did you lie, Tansy? I would have looked after you.'

She couldn't bear this. 'Leo, it's not——'

His strong teeth snapped together. 'You knew damned well that I wouldn't throw you to the wolves—God knows, I've behaved like a fool and a swine, but allow me a sense of responsibility, at least!'

She shrugged, desperate to get rid of him before her fragile composure broke and shattered. Bitterness propelled the next words. 'Yes, I'll allow you a sense of responsibility. I'm sure you'd have given me the money to look after it. Or for an abortion.'

'Damn you,' he said furiously, 'I'd have married you so fast——'

She was shaking her head, unable to think coherently because of the pain. 'There was no baby,' she said at last. 'I gave the piece that name because it was— convenient.'

Leo looked out over her head, clawing back his self-control. He said quietly, 'Convenient? Sometimes I think you're the most cold-blooded little bitch I've ever come across. Does a great gift feed on your life? Is everything grist to your mill?'

'Yes, it is!'

'You don't want anything permanent, do you, Tansy? You intend to spend the rest of your life worshipping at the altar of your muse. Marriage doesn't figure in your future at all—you made that perfectly clear. But you wanted to find out what passion was like. So you did, and then you ran back to your real life.'

She was already so pale that she couldn't lose any more colour, but at his words, an icy sweat seeped through her pores. 'What the hell else did you expect me to do?' she demanded.

His eyes burned into hers. Then he shrugged. 'Just what you did, I suppose.' He smiled cynically. 'I understood you better when I saw what you'd run from. I like the O'Briens, but you're wild and fey and so vividly alive that you look like a falcon in a nest of sparrows. It's not your fault that they weren't able to deal with someone like you; living with them must have stifled you.'

Astonished by his reading of the situation, she stared at him. He smiled derisively. 'And you're so bloody young! Far too young to be thinking of anything like a commitment. So I decided to let you run,' he said. 'I thought I'd give you your two years, and then I'd come and get you.'

She said quietly, 'What do you mean, give me my two years?'

He hesitated, eyes hooded as they scanned her face, but she had already turned away. 'I don't want to speak to you,' she said tonelessly.

He said, 'Get into the car.'

Automatically Tansy shook her head. He gave a low, angry laugh and took her arms, deposited her in the front seat and locked the door behind her. Her head came to rest on the back of the seat. Waves of exhaustion swept through her, carrying with them the temptation to let down her barriers and bawl like a frustrated child. But that would be a weakness, and she had never allowed herself such indulgences. So she sat quietly while he set the car in motion, her lacklustre eyes fixed on the high wooden houses, gay in their coats of paint, sliding by.

She didn't attempt to remonstrate, not even when they got to her new flat and he took the key and opened the door. Compared to the casual, leisured, moneyed charm of the Dacres' seaside house, it seemed soulless and transient.

'You look as though last night was too much for you,' he said quietly. 'I'll make you a cup of tea. Still only peppermint?' His tone was gently taunting.

She said wearily, 'There's some red zinger there if you'd rather have that.'

He laughed. 'I think I'll stick to peppermint, thanks.'

When he put the lemony red tea in front of her, she said, 'You've had someone watching me, haven't you?'

He said nothing.

Tansy's eyes flicked across the dark intentness of his face. 'Leo, please, don't lie to me. You didn't make any attempt to take me to the old address, and you didn't ask me where I was living now. You knew about the concert.'

'Yes.' He leaned back and looked at her with half-closed eyes, his expression oddly remote. 'I wanted to make things as easy for you as possible. No, listen to me. I lost you—you went away after Christmas and I didn't know where you were and I bloody near went frantic trying to find you. In the end you turned up in Queenstown. You'd bloody hitch-hiked there! Don't you ever do that again, do you hear me? I decided that wasn't ever going to happen again, so I made sure someone kept an eye on you.'

Tansy looked away. Her trembling hand was making little catspaws across the surface of her cup. 'I hate it,' she whispered. 'Being spied on and watched and manoeuvred like a puppet—you've done that to me all along, damn you. Next you'll be telling me that you organised the grant.'

His very impassivity gave him away.

'Why?' she whispered, closing her eyes to shut out the sight of his face, so dearly loved, so false.

'It wasn't payment for services rendered,' he said caustically. 'When I came down that first time I wanted to know what sort of person you were. Your background was—interesting. I was almost certain you knew where he was, and I was prepared to do anything necessary to persuade you to tell me. Then I met you, and every preconception was shot down. I was fascinated and intrigued, and to my astonishment I wanted you. The thought of you sleeping with my brother made me mad and jealous as hell.'

She said acidly, 'I did not sleep with him.'

'I know that now. But you wouldn't tell me anything, you wouldn't be bribed, even though your finances were pretty tenuous, and you wouldn't be charmed. The minute I mentioned Ricky's name I saw that you knew where he was, and I was worried sick about Grace.'

'How is she?' she asked swiftly.

'She's doing very well, so far. The op went off well, and the surgeon is hopeful. Ricky's made a hell of a difference, even though he's not the same son who went away. She's learning how to cope with the new Ricky. He's fine, too. He's a day boy at his old school, and is pulling out all the stops.' He said quite deliberately, 'When I met you my priority was Grace's health. But within a couple of days that had all changed. Unfortunately, you were completely obstructive. I could see how far an invitation to join us on the island would get, so I kidnapped you.'

'It was an outrageous thing to do!'

'Yes. Stupid, too, but I was desperate. Grace was dying before my eyes, lapsing into a lethargy that had her doctor worried sick. He told me that if something wasn't done she'd just wither away. I couldn't let that happen, Tansy, not even if it meant making you hate me.'

No, she could see that. In fact, she had always known that the driving force behind the whole affair was his loyalty to Grace, and his love for her.

She said, 'I was furious.'

'Weren't you just! I've never been slain with a look before. You made me furious, too, refusing to wear the few cheap jeans and T-shirts——'

'You must have known I wouldn't!'

'I hoped you would. I bought you those clothes because I wanted to dress you in silks and satins and lace and pearls—all the traditional things a lover buys. I tried to give you money because I couldn't bear to think of you worrying about it, scrimping and saving and struggling when I've got more than I know what to do with. But you wouldn't let me help you. I've never felt so useless in all my life.'

Agitation drove her to her feet. She walked across to the bookshelf and looked at the spines of the few books she owned. Three library books were stacked on their sides. She tried to read the titles but the words danced in the air. His words were clear and easily understood, but she was afraid to search beneath them for the subtext.

Did he want her to be his mistress, available whenever he came to Wellington? Keeping her head turned towards the books she said, 'And all the other things—the commission for the documentary——?'

'No. Oh, Tony Adams is a friend of mine, but when I dropped your name he already knew it. He'd heard one of your pieces last year, and slotted you away for future reference. No one would have commissioned you if your music weren't good.'

'That's a relief,' she muttered. At least she had that. Her brain raced, working out how soon she could afford to pay him the fake scholarship back. 'This place?' She didn't need an answer. She said, 'I'll repay——'

His hand on her shoulder was cruel and compelling. 'Don't say it,' he muttered as he swung her around. 'Don't even think it.'

Holding him off with two hands splayed against his chest, she asked clearly, 'Just what did you have in mind after the two years you gave me were up, Leo?'

'What I've had in mind since about the sixth time I saw you,' he said clearly. 'I want to marry you, Tansy.'

Her eyes widened enormously. 'Marry me?' She stared at him, seeing as though for the first time the strength in his face, the hard buccaneer's features.

'Yes. Don't say no, listen to me.' He spoke rapidly, using the splendid instrument of his voice to persuade. 'I know that women who marry and have families often don't live up to their potential. I couldn't bear it if you became a lesser person because I love you. But even before we made love, I knew that you were the most important person in the world to me. Making love was magical, like a vision of some other dimension, beyond anything I've ever experienced. It was for you, too, wasn't it?'

She nodded, half hypnotised by the mesmeric voice, the imperative crystalline gaze.

'Letting you go was the hardest thing I've ever done.' His expression altered. 'I was worried that you might be pregnant.'

'I wasn't,' she said swiftly. 'I swear, Leo, I wasn't.'

He looked at her. 'Then why the name of the requiem?'

She smiled. 'I wanted to be,' she said simply. 'I want your children. I want you. When I came back, I realised that I was never going to have another chance, and I grieved.'

'Tansy,' he said between his teeth, 'if you knew how I felt last night, seeing the name there—I wondered whether you'd had a miscarriage, and I wanted to be with you so much, to hold you, to comfort you—I've been in hell!'

'Good,' she said in a sharp little voice. 'You deserve to suffer!'

He flung his head back and laughed. 'I think that's what appealed to me at first,' he said. 'That sense of living on the edge, that stubborn refusal to be intimidated. You were so vital, so intense, and I wanted you.'

'You mean I was a challenge,' she snapped, her eyes flashing.

He grinned. 'Yes. I've always needed a challenge.'

Cold with anger, she tried to pull away. 'You used me. You were egotistical enough to think you could charm Rick's whereabouts from me, and then when that didn't work you kidnapped me.'

His fingers around her wrists were strong and merciless. He held her hands over his heart, so that she could feel the heavy pounding beneath her palms. In spite of her anger a slow tide of heat began to move through her.

'I took one look at you and everything went haywire.' His voice was savagely self-derisory, harsh with an emotion he didn't try to hide. 'You were different. You bypassed all the usual defences and homed straight in on to some part of me I didn't even know existed. I'd always wanted beauty in my lovers. But you weren't beautiful, at least not the first time I saw you. After that I didn't care. You were thin, and intense, and you blazed with such a fierce, white-hot fire that I was burned through to the bone. A street kid, an ex-prostitute, yet after that first afternoon I knew I was never going to forget you.'

'And you hated yourself for wanting a woman who'd been a prostitute. Well, all that emotion was wasted, because I was never on the streets,' she said coldly, and told him what had happened during that lost year.

He didn't seem surprised, but there was something in his face that made her take a hasty, involuntary step backwards. 'Why did you keep it a secret?' he asked in the lethal tone she had heard only once before.

She lifted her chin. 'Why shouldn't I? You had me already slotted into a niche, the tart made good; what business was it of yours?'

'Was it a test, Tansy? Did you want to know whether I could overlook your supposed past?'

Her curls spun wildly as she shook her head, but although she reacted spontaneously she found herself wondering whether perhaps unconsciously she had been setting traps for him. She had told herself that his probing into her past had been a violation of privacy, that he had no right, no need to know any more about her, but had she really wanted to discover whether a man like Leo Dacre, with power and privilege on his side, could fall in love with the woman he thought her to be?

She bit her lip. 'No,' she said, but even to herself her voice lacked conviction.

'I think it was. I think you deliberately withheld that bit of information from me, hoping it would keep me at a distance. It didn't work,' he said sardonically. 'I soon realised that no matter what had happened to you in the past, I didn't care. I was well and truly caught in that glittering web you spun——'

'Poor little fly,' she mocked, hurling the words at him like missiles. She stared at him, the blood running through her veins with a power and a purpose she hadn't felt since—since that night in his arms.

He caught a fistful of brilliant hair at the back of her head and held her still. His eyes gleamed, green as peridots, lit from within by gold. 'I can't let you go, Tansy. That's what you've reduced me to.'

'Don't you damned well blame me!' Her pulses were pounding heavily. 'You brought it on yourself! If you'd left me alone instead of harassing me and making my life a misery and kidnapping me—it's not even that you kidnapped me, it was the abuse of power. What the great Leo Dacre wanted done was done, even if you had to drag me all the way from Wellington to Auckland to do it. I knew I wasn't in any physical danger—but that's not the point.'

He held her gaze, his eyes suddenly ablaze. 'I know, and I'm sorry. I behaved like a bastard, and it serves me right if you refuse to have anything to do with me, but I'm not going to let it end like that! I'll be back—oh, I won't harass you, I'll just hope. Wherever you are, that's where I want to be,' he said slowly. 'I love you, Tansy. I want to marry you. Will you marry me?'

She didn't hesitate. 'Yes, I will. You're an egotistical, unscrupulous swine, but I love you too.'

He leaned over and put his fingers around hers, guiding her mug to safety. Then he stood up and pulled her into his arms, holding her very tight for a long time. After a while his chest lifted in an enormous sigh. 'Thank God,' he said devoutly.

She couldn't stop her laughter. Face buried in his chest, almost smothered, with the sound of his heart thudding in her ears, she could have sung with delight, with gratitude, with joy.

Instead she said dolefully, 'I'll never be a proper wife.'

'I rather like the idea of you being an improper one.'

'Damn it, Leo, you don't need someone who's only going to spend half her time in your world.'

He loosened his arms and tucked a strong finger under her chin, raising it until he could see her flushed face. 'I can hire someone to do the housework, someone to look after the kids if you decide you want some, someone to cook. I can buy people, Tansy. That's why the ones I can't buy are so precious. We'll talk about how we're going to organise our life together later; at the moment I'm just extremely relieved that there's going to be one.'

She glowered at him and asked incredulously, 'You mean—total surrender? Just like that? You take all of the fun out of it!'

His laughter was very tender. 'Don't you believe it. We've both got well-exercised egos, we'll fight and brawl and rapidly become notorious among our friends, but we'll talk, too. And we'll love each other until the day we die.'

She grinned, reached up, and kissed him. A couple of hours later she lifted her head from his chest and said sweetly, 'As long as we do that often, you'll probably be able to twist me around your little finger.'

'Mmm.' He ran a lean forefinger up her spine. 'I can't wait.'

Tansy settled back, relaxed and replete. She didn't try to fool herself that life with Leo would be peaceful and serene; he was right when he said they'd quarrel and brawl, and he was right, damn him, when he'd told her that her ego was as well-nourished as his. But oh, she thought, yawning and tilting her head so that her cheek rested on his shoulder, oh, it would be good. They would also talk and learn to adjust, make deals and try to master the subtle art of compromise. Whatever the future held, they would be together, and that was all that mattered.

PRIZE SURPRISE SWEEPSTAKES!

This month's prize:

BEAUTIFUL WEDGWOOD CHINA!

This month, as a special surprise, we're giving away a bone china dinner service for eight by Wedgwood**, one of England's most prestigious manufacturers!

Think how beautiful your table will look, set with lovely Wedgwood china in the casual Countryware pattern! Each five-piece place setting includes dinner plate, salad plate, soup bowl and cup and saucer.

The facing page contains two Entry Coupons (as does every book you received this shipment). Complete and return *all* the entry coupons; **the more times you enter, the better your chances of winning!**

Then keep your fingers crossed, because you'll find out by September 15, 1995 if you're the winner!

Remember: The more times you enter, the better your chances of winning!*

PRIZE SURPRISE
SWEEPSTAKES

OFFICIAL ENTRY COUPON

This entry must be received by: AUGUST 30, 1995
This month's winner will be notified by: SEPTEMBER 15, 1995

YES, I want to win the Wedgwood china service for eight! Please enter me in the drawing and let me know if I've won!

Name_____

Address _____ Apt. _____

City   State/Prov.   Zip/Postal Code

Account #_____

Return entry with invoice in reply envelope.

© 1995 HARLEQUIN ENTERPRISES LTD.   CWW KAL

PRIZE SURPRISE
SWEEPSTAKES

OFFICIAL ENTRY COUPON

This entry must be received by: AUGUST 30, 1995
This month's winner will be notified by: SEPTEMBER 15, 1995

YES, I want to win the Wedgwood china service for eight! Please enter me in the drawing and let me know if I've won!

Name_____

Address _____ Apt. _____

City   State/Prov.   Zip/Postal Code

Account #_____

Return entry with invoice in reply envelope.

© 1995 HARLEQUIN ENTERPRISES LTD.   CWW KAL

OFFICIAL RULES

PRIZE SURPRISE SWEEPSTAKES 3448

NO PURCHASE OR OBLIGATION NECESSARY

Three Harlequin Reader Service 1995 shipments will contain respectively, coupons for entry into three different prize drawings, one for a Panasonic 31" wide-screen TV, another for a 5-piece Wedgwood china service for eight and the third for a Sharp ViewCam camcorder. To enter any drawing using an Entry Coupon, simply complete and mail according to directions.

There is no obligation to continue using the Reader Service to enter and be eligible for any prize drawing. You may also enter any drawing by hand printing the words "Prize Surprise," your name and address on a 3"x5" card and the name of the prize you wish that entry to be considered for (i.e., Panasonic wide-screen TV, Wedgwood china or Sharp ViewCam). Send your 3"x5" entries via first-class mail (limit: one per envelope) to: Prize Surprise Sweepstakes 3448, c/o the prize you wish that entry to be considered for, P.O. Box 1315, Buffalo, NY 14269-1315, USA or P.O. Box 610, Fort Erie, Ontario L2A 5X3, Canada.

To be eligible for the Panasonic wide-screen TV, entries must be received by 6/30/95; for the Wedgwood china, 8/30/95; and for the Sharp ViewCam, 10/30/95.

Winners will be determined in random drawings conducted under the supervision of D.L. Blair, Inc., an independent judging organization whose decisions are final, from among all eligible entries received for that drawing. Approximate prize values are as follows: Panasonic wide-screen TV ($1,800); Wedgwood china ($840) and Sharp ViewCam ($2,000). Sweepstakes open to residents of the U.S. (except Puerto Rico) and Canada, 18 years of age or older. Employees and immediate family members of Harlequin Enterprises, Ltd., D.L. Blair, Inc., their affiliates, subsidiaries and all other agencies, entities and persons connected with the use, marketing or conduct of this sweepstakes are not eligible. Odds of winning a prize are dependent upon the number of eligible entries received for that drawing. Prize drawing and winner notification for each drawing will occur no later than 15 days after deadline for entry eligibility for that drawing. Limit: one prize to an individual, family or organization. All applicable laws and regulations apply. Sweepstakes offer void wherever prohibited by law. Any litigation within the province of Quebec respecting the conduct and awarding of the prizes in this sweepstakes must be submitted to the Regies des loteries et Courses du Quebec. In order to win a prize, residents of Canada will be required to correctly answer a time-limited arithmetical skill-testing question. Value of prizes are in U.S. currency.

Winners will be obligated to sign and return an Affidavit of Eligibility within 30 days of notification. In the event of noncompliance within this time period, prize may not be awarded. If any prize or prize notification is returned as undeliverable, that prize will not be awarded. By acceptance of a prize, winner consents to use of his/her name, photograph or other likeness for purposes of advertising, trade and promotion on behalf of Harlequin Enterprises, Ltd., without further compensation, unless prohibited by law.

For the names of prizewinners (available after 12/31/95), send a self-addressed, stamped envelope to: Prize Surprise Sweepstakes 3448 Winners, P.O. Box 4200, Blair, NE 68009.

RPZ KAL